Extract from Captain Stormfield's Visit to Heaven

Prometheus's Literary Classics Series

Henry Adams .... *Esther*
Aristophanes .... *Assembly of Women (Ecclesiazusae)*
Charles Brockden Brown ... *Wieland, or The Transformation*
Samuel Butler .... *Erewhon*
Lewis Carroll .... *Phantasmagoria*
Anton Chekov .... *Stories of Men*
Stories of Women
Kate Chopin .... *The Awakening*
Bayou Folk
Nigel Collins, compiler .... *Seasons of Life*
Stephen Crane .... *Maggie, A Girl of the Streets*
George Eliot .... *Scenes of Clerical Life*
Harold Frederic .... *The Damnation of Theron Ware*
Frank Harris .... *My Life and Loves*
Nathaniel Hawthorne ...... *The Scarlet Letter*
Henry James .... *The Turn of the Screw* and *The Lesson of the Master*
Ring Lardner Jr. .... *The Ecstasy of Owen Muir*
Sinclair Lewis .... *Babbitt*
Main Street
Jack London .... *The Star Rover*
Herman Melville .... *Battle-Pieces and Aspects of the War*
The Confidence Man
John Neal .... *Rachel Dyer*
Edgar Allan Poe .... *Eureka: A Prose Poem*
Sappho .... *The Love Songs of Sappho*
Upton Sinclair .... *The Moneychangers*
Henry David Thoreau ..... *Civil Disobedience, Solitude,* and *Life without Principle*
Leo Tolstoy .... *Classic Tales and Fables for Children*
Mark Twain .... *The Diaries of Adam and Eve*
Extract from Captain Stormfield's Visit to Heaven
The Man That Corrupted Hadleyburg
The Mysterious Stranger
Walt Whitman .... *Leaves of Grass*
Émile Zola .... *Lourdes*
Truth

Extract from Captain Stormfield's Visit to Heaven

Introduction by Victor Doyno

Mark Twain

LITERARY CLASSICS

59 John Glenn Drive
Amherst, New York 14228-2197

Published 2002 by Prometheus Books
59 John Glenn Drive, Amherst, New York 14228–2197.
VOICE: 716–691–0133, ext. 207. FAX: 716–564–2711.
WWW.PROMETHEUSBOOKS.COM

Extract from Captain Stormfield's Visit to Heaven originally published:
New York: Harper & Brothers, 1909.

Library of Congress Cataloging-in-Publication Data

Twain, Mark, 1835–1910.
Extract from Captain Stormfield's visit to heaven / Mark Twain ; introduction by Victor Doyno.
p. cm. — (Literary classics)
ISBN 1–59102–024–7 (alk. paper)
1. Ship captains—Fiction. 2. Voyages, Imaginary. 3. Heaven—Fiction. I. Title. II. Literary classics (Amherst, N.Y.)

PS1322 .E98 2002
813'.4—dc21 2002031843

Printed in the United States of America on acid-free paper

MARK TWAIN was born Samuel Langhorne Clemens in Florida, Missouri, on November 30, 1835, the son of John Marshall Clemens, an avowed freethinker, and his wife, Jane, a believer and connoisseur of the occult. These two opposing forces—freethought and spiritualism—colored the young Twain's view of the world and would later serve as material for his books.

As a child, Twain knew both violence and tragedy. In the town of Hannibal, Missouri, where he lived from 1839 to 1853, shootings and attempted shootings were not unusual events. Twain's older brother Benjamin died when Twain was only six; a few months later, the family lost their home to debt. When Twain was twelve, his father died.

It was at this time that Twain left school to go to work in order to help his financially strapped family, first as a printer's apprentice and later as a journeyman printer; he was also a river pilot, a prospector, and a roving newspaper reporter. Twain's journalistic travels took him throughout the United States as well as to South America, Europe, and the Middle East, from where he sent back entertaining travel letters. While a reporter for the Virginia City *Territorial Enterprise*, he adopted the pen name Mark Twain. His scathing, observant articles began to earn him a wide and loyal readership. Samuel Clemens/Mark Twain made his readers, and later his listeners during his lecture tours, familiar with his life: skillfully blending the real and the fictional, he created the character of Mark Twain whom Americans—and the world—recognized and loved in his many books, including *The Celebrated Jumping Frog of Calaveras County, and Other Sketches* (1867); *Innocents Abroad* (1869); *Roughing It* (1872); *The Adventures of Tom Sawyer* (1876); his masterpiece, *Adventures of Huckleberry Finn* (1884); and *The Man That Corrupted Hadleyburg* (1900).

Eulogized by William Dean Howells as "the Lincoln of our literature," Twain achieved great fame from his writing and earned a fortune. He lost this, however, following his involvement in a failed publishing house venture; thereafter, Twain lectured to clear his debts. The final two decades of Twain's life were marked, as were his first years, by a series of tragedies: during these years he lost in quick succession his beloved wife, Livy; a favorite nephew; his daughters Susy and Jean; and his sister, Pamela. Twain had toyed with the idea that life is a dream and that human emotions and experiences are delusions. His work at this time reflects his growing gloominess, pessimism, and contempt for organized religion: *Extracts from Adam's Diary* (1904) and *Eve's Diary* (1906) satirized Scripture; *Christian Science* (1907) ridiculed Mary Baker Eddy's new religion; *Extract from Captain Stormfield's Visit to Heaven* (1909) derided the belief in heaven. This is the period, too, of Twain's vitriolic *Letters from the Earth* (1906; first published in 1962) and *The Mysterious Stranger,* several versions of which were written during 1905–1906 and which was posthumously published in 1916. This and the other works of Twain's last years belie that popular image of the easy, affable American humorist; they reveal instead a man engaged in an often tortuous struggle to discover what life is and what meaning, if any, it holds.

Mark Twain died in Redding, Connecticut, on April 21, 1910.

INTRODUCTION

Sam Clemens/Mark Twain worked on the surprising idea of a "Visit to Heaven" for a very long time. His unconventional, challenging ideas about "heaven" undoubtedly would have shocked and offended many of his contemporaries! Sam Clemens's wife, Olivia Langdon Clemens, apparently wished that her husband would not publish the story. But he kept working on this concept—writing with his own unique blend of anarchy and discipline—for more than forty years.

After his wife died, Mark Twain published some of the manuscript in the December 1907 and January 1908 issues of *Harper's Magazine.* Perhaps he had wished to subvert the conventional Christmas-season religiosity. Then Twain again revised and published *Extract from Captain Stormfield's Visit to Heaven* in October 1909, as his last book released during his lifetime. We can think of this short book as the seventy-three-year-old Sam Clemens's/Mark Twain's honest, humorous, satirical farewell to his readers and to his world.

What is this concise book like? To many modern readers *Extract from Captain Stormfield's Visit to Heaven* now will seem both comical and quite provocative. This story combines Twain's usual easy readability and his surprising humor, while also containing material suitable for some polite, impolite, or rude debates with conventional believers in Christianity or other religions.

I. THE BOOK'S ORIGIN

We can explore three important originating influences: one very negative societal event, one negative literary source, and one very positive personal stroke of luck.

The idea for this book first came to Twain after the United States had endured a devastating civil war. By 1865 a total of about 1,446,000 men had served in the Union and Confederate armies. The American Civil War added to the country's normal rates of mortality by killing more than 618,000 men. In addition to these violent early deaths, at least 275,000 Northern and some unknown number of Southern soldiers suffered wounds. And some unfortunate noncombatants were also killed by the artillery shelling, as at Vicksburg. The quality of medical care at that time meant that many of the wounded would suffer continuing pain and also likely have a decreased life expectancy. We can reasonably calculate that these many dead and wounded people had families, parents, spouses, children, and siblings who would miss them and grieve for them. Within that much smaller population base the emotional impact would be, in contemporary terms, about equal to the loss of 423 people per day, a death toll about equal to two and a half Oklahoma City bombings per day for four and a half years. Or we can instead think of the American Civil War as creating, in sum, more total additional deaths than 250 September 11, 2001, World Trade Center attacks. If we calculate what the proportion of the Civil War deaths would be as against our present population, it would be about 17 million extra deaths. Moreover, the then-recent development of battlefield photography kept many Americans acutely aware of the massive human devastation. It seems probable that some survivors' and mourners' minds would have turned to wondering or dreaming about a loved person in a conventional Heaven.

In the mid-nineteenth century many conventional religious authorities thought in terms of a "God-centered heaven," a theologically oriented location or concept. But after the American Civil War, and increasingly in the English-speaking countries after the nineteenth- and twentieth-century wars, some religious thinking shifted to consider a human-centered Heaven. In November 1868 the novel *The Gates Ajar*, by Elizabeth Stuart Phelps, dealt with a young woman's grief for the battlefield death of her brother, with much attention to the consolation of her thoughts about her brother being alive in heaven; the initial printing quickly sold out. By 1888 the book had at least fifty-four subsequent printings. Apparently a great many people needed and read this book for personal consolation. Professor Nina Baym's book *Three Spiritualist Novels by Elizabeth Stuart Phelps* and Helen Sootin Smith's edition of *The Gates Ajar* (The Belknap Press of Harvard University Press, 1964) each offer a wealth of information about the era and about the theological controversies about "heaven."

But Mark Twain did not believe in a "heaven," and he wished to explore and attack the concept. Twain clearly did not use *The Gates Ajar* as a line-by-line source or as a series of topics. Instead, that book served him as a negative influence, as an irritant, as an example of what forms of illusional thinking he wished to combat. As the noted Twain scholar Alan Gribben has explained in his *Mark Twain's Library*, vol. 2, in October 1870 Twain published two poems in *The Galaxy* that use and mock the idea of the gates or doors of heaven being left slightly open. (When Sam Clemens/Mark Twain published this two-poem exchange, his wife, Livy, was in the last trimester of her first pregnancy. She almost miscarried in October 1870. At that time, of course, neither parent could have known that Langdon would live only nineteen months. The topic of a dead infant would become highly emotional, not funny, and quite personal for the young couple.) The first of these poems may have been written by a conventional, polite male poet, but I suggest that Twain may have himself written the mockingly realistic four-stanza reply, as if it was spoken by the supposed guardian of the heavenly gates, Saint Peter:

THE GATES AJAR

On the occasion of the birth of his first child the poet writes:

One night, as old Saint Peter slept,
He left the door of Heaven ajar,
When through a little angel crept
And came down with a falling star.

One summer, as the blessed beams
Of morn approached, my blushing bride
Awakened from some pleasing dreams
And found that angel by her side.

God grant but this, I ask no more,
That when he leaves this world of sin,
He'll wing his way to that bright shore
And find the door of Heaven again.

Whereupon Saint Peter, not liking this imputation of carelessness, thus (by a friend) replies:

ON THE PART OF THE DEFENCE.

For eighteen hundred years and more
I've kept my door securely tyled;*
There has no little angel strayed,
No one been missing all the while.

I did not sleep as you supposed,
Nor leave the door of Heaven ajar,
Nor has a little angel strayed
Nor gone down with a falling star.

Go ask that blushing bride and see
If she don't frankly own and say,
That when she found that angel babe,
She found it in the good old way.

God grant but this, I ask no more,
That should your numbers still enlarge,
You will not do as heretofore,
And lay it to old Peter's charge.[1]

I find it mildly amusing that Twain may have adopted the pose of being either Saint Peter's friend or a friend of the editor of the column in the magazine. We can safely assume that Twain disliked the first poem's coy denial of human sexuality, by asserting in the reply that the woman found the baby in the "good old way."

In addition, Twain's nonpoetic, unmistakable prose remarks about *The Gates Ajar* certainly leave no doubt about his attitudes. In 1868 Twain stated that he had written a version of *Captain Stormfield*, saying, "I had turned it into a burlesque of The Gates Ajar, a book which had imagined a mean little ten-cent heaven about the size of Rhode Island—a heaven large enough to accommodate about a tenth of one percent of the

*I.e., "tied" or "tiled," "protected from intrusion"

Christian billions who had died in the past nineteen centuries. I raised the limit." Mark Twain's use of a poker or gambling phrase—"I raised the limit"—indicates that he did not have an attitude of polite, religious sanctimoniousness toward "heaven." And in 1897 Twain mentioned: "Capt. Stormfield's visit to Heaven? (Begun in 1867–8 as a satire upon the 'Gates Ajar' & still in MS)." In 1906 Twain said to Isabel Lyon that this work was intended "as a satire on 'The Gates Ajar.'" As we read and reread this comedic work we can understand how combative Twain's mind was. He enjoyed using the conventional ideas, props, and concepts of heaven to undermine completely any beliefs in the religious notion.

Twain's creative process made a very important, great leap forward because of a surprisingly important boat trip. In 1866 Twain embarked on the "opposition line" ship *America*, headed from San Francisco to Nicaragua. The notebook Twain kept during this voyage reveals that he wrote comments about at least three significant topics: the distinctive personality or precise character of the ship's captain, an increased knowledge of deaths and burials at sea, and the treatment of a Jewish man. These three topics would eventually each exert a significant influence upon this story.

Mark Twain's first and strongest impressions involved the ship's most unusual commander. Captain Edgar (Ned) Wakeman was a gruff, strong, experienced, highly opinionated seaman. This man held many unconventional ideas. He could swear marvelously, and he could and would make up biblical quotations and "facts" quickly and recklessly in order to defeat any hapless or surprised debate opponents. Twain liked this man immensely, noticing that the captain had the earnestness and talkativeness of a sailor who had spent much time alone. Shortly after they left San Francisco, the ship immediately faced a severe storm. One passenger who had already served fourteen years at sea made a remark that Twain jotted in his notebook, "...if anybody can save her its old Wakeman."

And Twain made many more observations in his notebook, indicating that the captain was engaging his imagination. Sometime after his notebook entry for around midnight, December 22, 1866, Twain wrote:

> I had rather travel with that old portly, hearty, jolly, boisterous, good-natured old sailor, Capt Ned Wakeman than with any other man I ever came across. He never drinks, & never plays cards; he never swears,

> except in the privacy of his own quarters, with a friend or so, & then his feats of fancy blasphemy are calculated to fill the hearer with awe and <the liveliest>* admiration. His yarns—
>
> Just as I got that far, Capt. W. came in, sweating & puffing—for we are off the far southern coast of Mexico, & the weather is a little sultry....[2]

Sam Clemens, a highly competent former riverboat pilot, may have felt almost overwhelmed by Wakeman's forceful, extraordinary personality.

Mark Twain certainly also felt fascinated by precisely how the man spoke. By the second or third day of the voyage, Twain devoted a great deal of time to capturing the sound, rhythm, vocabulary, and commanding presence of the man by writing in his notebook a fictional rendition, or a semitranscription, of how the captain had described a ride in a runaway horse carriage using his own familiar—but inappropriate—sailor's vocabulary. I regard this little-known speech as a tour de force for a writer (this transcription does not preserve all the revisions):

> Cap W —— Riding in a carriage! Belay! Don't talk to me about riding in a carrage—I got enough of that, with Hill—in Newburyport, twenty years ago, now, I reckon.
>
> We went to the livery concern—it was Sunday morning & I was stove in, wore out, crippled up, with all the different kinds of rheumatics you can find in the medicine books—& Hill chartered a horse for the voyage, & a <flim> clean clipper-built concern for to carry the passengers—but I <says,> said
>
> 'Look-a-here! Are you the chief mate of this establishment?—because I want you to understand that I'm a cripple—I can't move hand nor foot, & I want a horse that *one* man can steer, do you see?'
>
> And he says 'Here, take out that horse & put in this one—black, the first one was, & wicked—stood up with his figure-head in the clouds—white the last one, but wicked, too, I judged—anyway I didn't hardly like the cut of his jib—& I said as much to Hill—I said, "Here, now, take some of that rattlin' stuff [perhaps a leather-strap with bells attached] & reeve it through his fair-leaders there forrard, & seize it onto his fore-ancle, so as if we got in a tight place & he missed stays or

*The arrow brackets indicate Twain's manuscript cancellation.

> run away we could fetch him up with a round turn—couldn't do much on 3 legs I don't suppose?"
>
> But no,—*I* didn't know anything about it, Hill knowed it all. So we cast <loose> off & got under way, /stood out to wind'ard & it was all fair sailing till we sighted a fleet of sheep or something or other of that kind, & then bloody murder how he did shake out his reefs and howl before the wind! Go?—go ain't no name for it!—over gardens & orchards & dogs & cats, curb-stones & children—round this corner & then around that—everybody yelping, everybody skurrying out of the way, nobody trying to stop him—I says "Luff, in the name o' God! & let him go about!—because I see right ahead of us a little cove with a bulkhead across the other end of it—& Hill he put her down hard-a-port—but it was too late—it warn't no use—she missed stays & down she went like a rocket into that cove & fetched up like the staving of a ship-of-the-line agin that d——d bulkhead!—and out we went & Hill & me—I was on the port side & the minute she struck she swung, broadside on, & I went over that bulkhead like a shot & Hill cleared the starboard bulwarks & struck on his shoulder & scoured the harness off of him & peeled the hide, too, & the horse—hell! there warn't enough of him left to hold an inquest on! shaking like a sick monkey on a lee back-stay. . . .[3]

Twain must have loved the rapid flow, the uninterrupted tumble of sailing terms applied to a barely understood—and minimally understandable—horse accident. The narrating captain does not accept any blame; he is so self-confident that he does not realize that the unusual attempt to tie a noisy extra line on the horse's foot may have contributed to the accident. Letting the horse "Luff" would mean dropping the reins and letting the frightened, runaway horse have no direction. But the shouted inappropriate directions, the rollover carriage crash, and the ejected passengers pour like lava out of Wakeman's mouth. Twain may have been fascinated by this commanding, sincere, self-confident, earnest, highly verbal narrator; this man felt fully confident and did not censor what he said. Perhaps Twain felt, at some point, the challenge of capturing the man's voice and unconventional vitality in print.

But Twain also observed and captured a contrasting side of the captain's way of speaking. The ship had much severe sickness on it, and Twain jotted in his notebook how serious, direct, terse, and controlled Captain

Wakeman's speech could be when he had to deal with a bad situation. Twain's notebook entry describes a memorably difficult moment, the captain's human consideration, and nature's way of dealing with death:

> Christmas Eve—9 P.M. Me and the Capt & Kingman out forward—
>
> Capt. said—Don't like the looks of that point with the mist outside of it—hold her a point free.
>
> Quartermaster (touching his hat)—The child is dead sir."
>
> <Wh> (Been sick 2 days.—) What are yr orders.
>
> Capt. Tell Ben to send the Dr. for the parson to speak to the grandmother and the mate to speak to the young mother—bury at sea at daylight or preserve in spirits & bury at St Juan (depart)
>
> Capt.—Store-keeper don't you know you are out of your place here forward with the officers on watch—nobody ever tell you that?
>
> S—No sir?
>
> C—Well, it ought to have been the first thing told & you wouldnt have made any mistake (Departure of S)
>
> D—arrived and C told him to find out wishes of mother.
>
> C—If it was mine I'd preserve it cost what it might—but poor thing—God's will be done.
>
> Mate wh. Mother—Madam, you say the grandmother wants it buried at sea at daylight—right—but you have yr say—whatever you wish *that* shall be done. (Exit) (11 AM. tomorrow—C—Enter in log–died at 9 PM.
>
> Had sharks, whales, porpoises, dolphins—purser (Dodge's) phosphorescents—70 miles.[4]

Much of the captain's language seems quite controlled, and he may be forgiven his deflective, psychologically useful, abrupt rebuke to the storekeeper, immediately followed by his gentler explanation. Both the experienced sailors, mate and Captain, seem to be against burial at sea. Twain thought that he had observed sharks—very unlikely to be visible that late at night in December—but then softened the observation by adding the more obvious fishes. Although most nineteenth-century references to sharks following a ship refer to the slave ships coming from Africa to America, this reference combines, in a threatening way, important topics: the celebration of the birth of an innocent, religiously significant child; death at sea of a Caucasian child; familial grief; and sharks.

If a dead child would be attacked by sharks, how would the innocent, undeserving child victim appear in "heaven"? Or, with a more general focus and phrasing, should a realistic adult expect any justice in "heaven"? When we read this notebook entry we are at some depth in Twain's observant, perceptive mind. Twain's creative mind must have responded well to the captain's self-control and his range of emotions.

By the time the story would be fully developed Twain would have many of Captain Stormfield's speeches sound rapid and emphatic—the way that the excited, enthusiastic, observant captain would speak about the runaway horse. And Twain could also use the man's commanding tone of voice to explain about "heaven," with some of the more complex explanations stated by one of the captain's friends, an additional, calm, experienced man named Sandy, a character who takes on the role of an explainer, a conversational partner who knows all about "heaven."

Twain was fortunate enough to have made that one voyage with Wakeman in 1866 from San Francisco to Nicaragua and then to have seen him again in Panama in 1868. When Twain wrote part of *Roughing It*, he described "the Old Admiral" as a "roaring terrific combination of wind and lightning and thunder." On one quite fortunate occasion, probably in 1868, Wakeman confided to Twain that he had dreamed about visiting Heaven. The combination of Wakeman's unusual, forceful, authoritative personality and the notion of a descriptive travelogue to "Heaven" gave Twain the precious combination of a perfect narrator-personality and a rich satiric target. In fact, the narrator's powerful authoritative personality helps create a more persuasive, imaginative, intellectual travel book.

During that first, highly influential voyage Twain also made some other notebook memoranda about a Jewish character named Solomon, who had actually suffered some cruel mistreatment from the crew and passengers during the trip. But by the time Twain's sympathetic, creative consciousness had written about the man, Twain had decided to have Captain Stormfield become quite emotional in reaching out toward the suffering man. (See section 4 below.)

Twain's mind toyed with the many different possibilities over the years. In 1878 he wrote out a notebook entry that captures the flavor of his thought and his enthusiasm:

> Have all sorts of heavens—have a gate for each sort.
>
> One gate where they receive a barkeeper with military salutes, swarms of angels in the sky & a noble torch-light procession. *He* thinks he is *the* lion of Heaven. Procession over, he drops at once into awful obscurity. But the roughest part of it is, that he has to do 30 weeks penance–day and night he must carry a torch, and shout himself hoarse, to do honor to some poor scrub whom he wishes had gone to hell.
>
> Wakeman visits these various heavens.
>
> W. is years & years in darkness, between solar systems.
>
> (March 20, 1878)

Clearly Twain's creative imagination was developing and probing the idea of an admirable narrator who resembled Captain Wakeman in forcefulness and in blasphemy skills.

2. Connotations, Then and Now

Let us simply examine a few meanings that the seven title words would have carried for Twain and for his earliest readers, rather as if we were carefully unwrapping some intricately packed gifts. The word "Extract" could, of course, carry at least three relevant meanings; this word could certainly refer to a selection of carefully chosen samples from a larger body of writings, and the word might also refer to a strong, but quite essential part of a chemical or liquid, as in a lemon or licorice "extract." The notion of an "extract" also has specific meanings for some written ideas, ranging from "a pithy summary" or "an outline" to a legal term for "the proper written evidence that can be used for future decisions." And after Twain had worked on the project repeatedly, his late decision to use the word "Extract" might also have carried some personal connotations of frustration, as if to say, "Because I've done a great deal of good thinking and phrasing on this topic, here is a short, indicative sample."

As indicated, Twain took over the notion of a traveling, commenting sea captain, and the author gave his main narrator the character of an unquestionable decisive authority, a blunt, self-confident, observant, intelligent, forceful speaker. Twain used this narrator's personality to place many then-controversial or shocking ideas in the public arena, and this author would not expect that any readers would try to contradict or disagree with this unusual, highly individualistic, commanding "Captain."

The name "Stormfield" evolved over time, through at least seven surviving separate manuscript segment drafts. The names for the narrating captain may provide some sense of Twain's changing, developing purposes. In all probability Twain might have liked the real name "Wakeman" because it implied a man who was, indeed, already awakened, not thoughtlessly "sleeping" through his life with the conventional, societally shared, unquestioned preconceptions about religion and an afterlife. Twain had one early draft with a title page: "Captain Wakeman's Travels to Heaven." (But this name could have led to some confusion because Twain also knew and respected a newspaper journalist, George Wakeman, who died in 1870.) Another version of the story was called "The Travels of Captain Eli Stormfield, Mariner in Heaven," and one version was titled and revised "From Captain Stormfield's <Account> Reminiscences." Similarly Twain named and retitled one version "Captain Stormfield's <Journey> Visit to Heaven." I think that Twain felt drawn toward the name "Stormfield" because the combination implied, or carried a coded name for, an open location for tempestuous or stormy intellectual debates. It also seems worthy of mention that Twain named his last house "Stormfield" in 1908, perhaps because the money from the original publication of this work contributed to finishing his final home, and perhaps because from that residence Twain and his visitors could see storms approaching from every direction.

Over the years Twain had tested out many words for this antireligious, intellectual voyage: "Travels," "Journey," "Account," and "Reminiscences." The concept of a "Visit" would seem quite normal for a world-traveling sea captain, a talkative man who may have already arrived at and commented upon many exotic places. Moreover, the word also implies that the narrator can die and return to life, that this speaker has had the unusual "good fortune" of dying only temporarily, and that the speaker cares enough and is tough and generous enough to return to tell the truth to us, the living. The combined connotations of a "Visit" and a "Captain" unite to create some greater credibility, reliability, or supposed truthfulness for these once astonishingly unconventional ideas. The combination of a "Visit to Heaven" implies a return to earth as a living, sentient, observant, evaluative, informative traveler.

But the complete title actually serves to undermine completely any notions of religious mystery, secretiveness, and sanctity. Moreover, Captain Stormfield's "Heaven" turns out to be a relatively democratic place to visit, with many human merits given genuine recognition, while many conventional, unquestioned religious expectations, such as angels' wings, harps, and singing, are treated as the targets of sharp satire. Of course Twain did not himself believe in "heaven," but he very much enjoyed toying with the idea.

The concept of "heaven" demands a great deal more information. First of all, some contemporary Christians will be surprised to learn that several religions do not believe in any heaven or afterlife. Aristotle thought that many polytheistic religions believed that the many gods lived in the highest places in the universe. The Islands of the Blessed, Elysium, Tartarus, Valhalla, and similar places were thought to be the locations of the gods and of some fortunate deceased humans, while a locational opposition, such as Shoel or Hades or Hell, was reserved for the bad or evil. The Mohammedan belief involves a seven-step progression from the near-earthly to the Abode of the Most High, while the Buddhist belief posits a loss of all earthly desires in Nirvana.

Many early Christian beliefs built on an idea of a union of "the just" or "blessed souls" with God, an unclouded vision of the most High. Christian belief systems evicted Zeus and the other classical gods and goddesses from "heaven," repopulating heaven with a "God," in single or tripartite form. For this belief system, a shared presence with or spiritual proximity to the Divine would be a Heavenly State, a *Paradiso.* Supposedly, at some future time a general resurrection of all souls would begin a Millenium in which God and the Saints, and the souls of the faithfully departed would live and reign on Earth and in Heaven. For centuries Christian children and adults have been taught some version or blend of these ideas.

But as the knowledge systems changed from an Earth-centered view to a Sun-centered conception of the solar system, the understandings of astronomy, optical improvements, and telescopic measurements called much of the earlier Christian religious worldview into question. The shift from an Earth-centered to a Sun-centered universe was destructive to the old beliefs. Copernicus thought through a heliocentric universe; Galileo in 1609–1630 used telescopic astronomy to learn; by 1687 Isaac

Newton's publications gave coherence to the new structure of the universe. Uranus was discovered by William Herschel (1781), and Neptune was discovered by Urbain Leverrier and by John Couch Adams (1846). No reputable scientist has thus far discovered a location for "heaven." Now, in 2002, few if any educated people would suggest a physical location for "heaven" in this universe.

Apparently the current scientific consensus would state that we live on a planet that revolves around a medium-size star which is located near the edge of an average-size galaxy in a group of about nineteen other galaxies in a universe that contains some unknown total number of galaxies, perhaps as many as one hundred billion other galaxies. Moreover, this Earth has been in existence about 10,000 times longer than our race of *Homo sapiens.* Our universe apparently is at least three times the age of our planet. Our conventional notions about "heaven" may be only figments of human imagination, only useful for stimulating human thinking.

Many important examples of mythic literature deal with a hero's journey to the afterworld (usually the underworld) and with the adventurer's return to the land of the living to explain how the earth, the gods, and an afterlife function. Twain's version has a puzzled, officious gatekeeper for heaven, but no magical weapons or threatening demons. Twain's imagination of "heaven" offers a humorously democratic, oddly individualistic meritocracy. The values of Twain's deliberately disbelieved "heaven" would be challenging to and subversive of traditional religions.

3. Clemens's/Twain's Personal and Familial Meanings

This concept also held several additional, intensely personal meanings for Sam Clemens because he and his family had to face a series of losses to death. The author's own disbelief in "heaven" may have made these events and the necessary postdeath familial conversations particularly painful and difficult. In the America of the 1860s to the 1910 era and even later an atheist would almost certainly feel relatively lonely because sharing his or her real opinions about death and heaven might provoke shock, isolation, or anger from loved ones.

Sam Clemens had become close to his wife's father, Jervis Langdon; but this generous abolitionist and famous man suffered a long, losing battle with stomach cancer from the spring to the late summer in 1870. In addition, after Sam Clemens and Livy Langdon became married, her close friend Emma Nye came to visit them in Buffalo, New York; but Miss Nye soon came down with typhoid fever and, after a month, died in the Clemenses' Buffalo home at 472 Delaware Avenue. The Clemenses' firstborn child, Langdon, weighed only about four and a half pounds when he arrived on November 7, 1870. The child was sickly, and he died in Hartford, Connecticut, on June 2, 1872. The next two Clemens children, Susy and Clara, would play a game inside their Hartford home about an angel coming down from heaven to take up a dead baby, and Susy once inquired how the dead baby would know the family in heaven, because he had been so little when he died.

We should gauge how lonely Sam Clemens/Mark Twain must have felt in his atheistic beliefs, in his disbelief about heaven. Within his own family he was surrounded by loved people who believed in "heaven." In July 1885 his wife, Livy, made a note in her diary "wondering" whether a recently deceased friend of the Langdon family, Mrs. Henry Sage of Ithaca, would be able to "see father and tell him all about us." Of course, Livy would have wanted her father to know of the births of her children and about how they grew.

Sam Clemens and his wife also suffered the totally unexpected death of their oldest daughter, Susy, in August 1896. Sam and Livy were in Italy, expecting that Susy would arrive about August 12. Instead they learned of the illness, spinal meningitis, that ultimately caused her death in Hartford on August 18. The letters by Clemens/Twain and his very good friend, William Dean Howells, reveal how these two highly intelligent men grappled with Susy's death and with the conventional religious consolations.

Howells wrote to Clemens on September 13, 1896. When reading this letter we should understand that Howells and his wife had previously suffered a similar death of their child, Winnie. Accordingly, Howells's consolation was heartfelt and sincere, building upon the words Clemens had given the Howells family during their sorrows:

Far Rockaway, L.I. Sept. 13, 1896

My dear Clemens:

I remember how you came in one day when we were bleeding from the death of Winnie, and said to me, "Oh did I *wake* you?" because I suppose my heavy heart had got into my eyes, and I looked sleep-broken. I have never forgotten just how you said it, and the tender intelligence you put into your words, and I wish now my affection for you and your wife could translate itself into some phrase that could be as nearly like comfort. There is really nothing to say to you, poor souls, and yet I must write, as I have already written to Mrs. Clemens to say that we suffer with you. As for the gentle creature who is gone, the universe is all a crazy blunder if she is not some where in conscious blessedness that knows and feels your love. The other night I woke to think, "Why do we bother trying to conceive a state of being beyond this which shall be different from this, when there will really be nothing but something like an earthly separation to bridge over?" You are parted from her a little longer and that's all, and the joint life will go on when you meet on the old terms, but with the horror and pain gone forever. This is the easiest and the most reasonable thing to believe, and it is not to be refused because it is so old and simple.

We join in the love to you which has known the same sorrow as yours.

W. D. Howells.[5]

Howells certainly sincerely wished to offer emotional comfort and some hope of seeing Susy again. His letter conveys and reaffirms the terms of conventional consolation, with the hopes of remeeting the loved one. Moreover, Howells's letter mentions conceiving "a state of being beyond this which shall be different from this." Of course Twain had been and would continue imaging "a state of being beyond this," but Twain's "heaven" was a sarcasm.

Sam Clemens/Mark Twain replied from his courteous, grateful, but opposing point of view, writing to Howells on September 24, 1896. As we read over this anguished letter, we may forgive some of Clemens's excessive, self-centered grief comparisons and notice some small signs of obsessive/compulsive attention to detail and to ironically cruel coincidence:

Dear Howells:

Yes, you two know what we feel—but no others among our friends. They have lost children, but the proportions were not the same. As Mrs. Clemens says, "they have lost a daughter, but they have not lost a Susy Clemens." There was not a detail of Susy's make-up that was commonplace.

To me our loss is bitter, bitter, bitter. Then what must it be to my wife. It would bankrupt the vocabularies of all the languages to put it into words. For the relation between Susy & her mother was not merely & only the relation of mother & child, but that of sweethearts, lovers also. "Do you love me, momma?" "No, I don't love you, Susy, I worship you."

What a ghastly tragedy it was; how cruel it was; how exactly & precisely it was planned; & how remorselessly every detail of the dispensation was carried out. Susy stood on the platform at Elmira at half past ten on the 14th of July, 1895, in the glare of the electric lights, waving her good-byes as our train moved westward on the long trip; & she was brimming with life & the joy of it. That is what I saw; & it was what her mother saw through her tears. One year, one month, & one week later, Livy & Clara had completed the circuit of the globe, arriving at Elmira at the same hour in the evening, by the same train & *in the same car*—& Susy was there to meet them—lying white & fair in her coffin in the house she was born in.

They were flying on the wings of steam & in the torture of dread and anxiety; & if three little days could have been spared them out of the rich hoard laid up for the building of the coming ages, poor Susy would have died in her mother's arms—& the poor three days were denied; they could not be afforded.

(Blank to be filled in some day.)

We send our love to both of you. Mrs. Clemens asks me to thank Mr. Howells for his note, & to say that it was a comfort to her, coming as it did from a heart that had suffered the same bruise as her own.

Good-bye. Will healing ever come, or life have value again?

And shall we see Susy? Without doubt! Without *shadow* of doubt, if it can furnish opportunity to break our hearts again.

S. L. Clemens[6]

Perhaps Clemens thought of later filling in his own unusual blank space in his letter with his extended, obsessive thoughts about the cruel coincidence or with his imagined thoughts about how devastatingly hard it would have been for Livy to embrace Susy as the daughter died. Significantly, Sam Clemens reveals, in the third paragraph before the closing, that Howells's letter of consolation had helped only his wife. Clemens precisely and silently implies by his own omission of a parallel gratitude that he himself did not find or could not accept any similar conventional consolation. Moreover, Clemens also implicitly rejects the usual idea of ever seeing Susy again, unless it would be to repeat or extend the crushing sadness. This letter was clearly written by a sensitive, self-controlling, precise, emotionally devastated father who could not believe in the conventional notions of "heaven." I infer that Sam Clemens/Mark Twain must have been a strong, courageous, determined man to have continued his dedicated, argumentative writing against the idea of "heaven."

Such sorrow would recur years later, in June of 1904, when Livy died. Sam Clemens's letter to Howells was written the first day after her death:

> Dear Howells:
>
> Last night at 9.20 I entered Mrs. Clemens's room to say the usual good-night—& she was dead! tho' no one knew it. She had been cheerfully talking, a moment before. She was sitting up in bed—she had not laid down for months—& Katie & the nurse were supporting her. They supposed she had fainted, & they were holding the oxygen pipe to her mouth, expecting to revive her. I bent over her & looked in her face, & I think I spoke—I was surprised and troubled that she did not notice me. Then we understood, & our hearts broke. How poor we are to-day!
>
> But how thankful I am that her persecutions are ended. I would not call her back if I could.
>
> To-day, treasured in her worn old Testament, I found a dear & gentle letter from you, dated Far Rockaway, Sept. 13, 1896, about our poor Susy's death. I am tired & old; I wish I were with Livy.
>
> I send my love—& hers—to you all.
>
> S L C.[7]

Howells wrote back to Clemens immediately, saying:

> My dear Clemens:
>
> The news has just reached us. I will not try to say anything in the stupid notion of trying to help you. But I must, as if it had never

> occurred to me before, realize in words, that the character which now remains a memory, was one of the most perfect ever formed on the earth. How often John and I have spoken of the wonderful goodness, that soul of exquisite kindness, which was so strong and so gentle! Poor old fellow; I am so sorry for you and your girls. But they will have the comfort of taking up her place in your life. What nonsense! Even they can not do that. Well, here are my love and pity.
>
> Yours ever
>
> W. D. Howells.[8]

Intriguingly, Howells offered a form of conventional consolation, but immediately corrected himself, recognizing his own "nonsense!"

Sam Clemens replied to his close friend's letter, giving a glimpse into the depth of his sorrow:

> Dear Howells:
>
> We have to sit & hold our hands and wait—in the silence and solitude of this prodigious house.... We excuse ourselves from all the friends that call—though of course only intimates come. Intimates—but they are not the old old friends, the friends of the old old times when we laughed. Shall we ever laugh again? If I could only see a dog that I knew in the old times! & could put my arms around his neck & tell him all, everything, & ease my heart....
>
> It was too pitiful, these late weeks, to see the haunting fear in her eyes, fixed wistfully upon mine, & hear her say, as pleading for denial & heartening, "You don't think I am going to die, do you? Oh, I don't want to die." For she loved her life, and so wanted to keep it.
>
> S L C.[9]

Sam Clemens/Mark Twain lived more than five years after writing this letter. I infer that after Livy's death it must have been extraordinarily difficult for this man to write with humor about any postdeath state. And I infer that Twain must have had a strong devotion to his readers to even think of continuing working on the idea of a visit to "heaven."

4. Twain's Creative and Philosophical Decisions

Over the years Twain wrote and rewrote, creating and revising his ideas and phrasings. For example, Twain once wrote a version that included Captain Stormfield's self-characterization as, at first, an anti-Semite, but a prejudiced man who sincerely and immediately changes based on his simple human responsiveness to another person's grief. In an early manuscript version, Captain Stormfield sees another space-traveler and welcomes the man aboard. While the men become acquainted Captain Stormfield explains and convinces his new passenger, Solomon Goldstein, that, based on Stormfield's life, they are both likely bound for hell. Solomon quickly internalizes this information and immediately starts to cry because he fears that he will never again see his dead daughter, who could not ever be in hell. Captain Stormfield responds clumsily, earnestly, with strong human empathy:

> ...he didn't need to keep his sorrows to himself any more, he could pour them right into my heart, which was wide open and ready; and he did; till it seemed to me I couldn't bear it....She was his pet, his playfellow, the apple of his eye; she was ten years old, and dead six months, and he was glad to die himself, so he could have her in his arms again....And here, in that father's heart that hope was dead....

Captain Stormfield has such sincere compassion for the man that he tells us:

> ..."I wish I was bound for heaven and could trade places with him, so he could see his child, damned if I wouldn't do it." If ever you are situated like that, you will understand the feeling.

Twain had the anguish and imagination to have his sincere, gruff sea captain extend genuine human sorrowful compassion, even extending to the point of supposed self-sacrifice, self-substitution. Obviously it would have been impossible for Sam Clemens/Mark Twain to publish this episode while his wife was alive. I suggest that this manuscript passage establishes that Sam Clemens fully felt the positive appeal of a fictional "heaven," but was intellectually unable to give the notion any credence.

Twain clearly had an extraordinary devotion to this project. He certainly wished to present his complex, unconventional, humorous, and sarcastic ideas to his readers. He placed a version in *Harper's Magazine* that indicates how carefully and earnestly he considered his work. At one point, near the ending of Part I, Twain playfully explored the idea that people could be any age they wished to be in "heaven." That late, penultimate, magazine version had a concluding section to Part I in which Captain Stormfield and his friend Sandy, the fictional good debating companion, discuss what ages and levels of wisdom people can have in heaven. Sandy had been explaining to Captain Stormfield how people who had died young could reach some age of wisdom in heaven, and Stormfied replies:

> "Look here," says I, "do you know what you're doing?"
>
> "Well, what am I doing?"
>
> "You are making heaven pretty comfortable in one way, but you are playing the mischief with it in another."
>
> "How you talk! Would heaven be heaven if you couldn't slander folks?"
>
> "Come to think, I don't believe it would—for some people—but I hadn't thought of it before."
>
> "For 'some people'? There you hit it. The trouble on earth is, that they leave out the *some-people* class—they try to fix up a heaven for only one kind of people. It won't work. There's all kinds here—and God cares for all kinds. He makes all happy; if He can't do it in one way, He does it in another. He doesn't leave anybody out in the cold."[10]

But Twain significantly revised for the 1909 book version. Twain canceled everything after "...but you are playing the mischief with it in another." Apparently Twain had decided that the rest of his work already contained enough relativistic individuation in "heaven."

Instead, Twain created and inserted a strongly emotional passage, a section that conveys both husbandly empathy and deep sorrow for the human condition:

> ["You are making heaven pretty comfortable in one way, but you are playing the mischief with it in another."]
>
> "How d' you mean?"

> "Well," I says, "take a young mother that's lost her child, and—"
>
> "Sh!" he says. "Look!"
>
> It was a woman. Middle-aged, and had grizzled hair. She was walking slow, and her head was bent down, and her wings hanging limp and droopy; and she looked ever so tired, and was crying, poor thing! She passed along by, with her head down, that way, and the tears running down her face, and didn't see us. Then Sandy said, low and gentle, and full of pity:
>
> "*She's* hunting for her child! No, *found* it, I reckon. Lord, how she's changed! But I recognized her in a minute, though it's twenty-seven years since I saw her. A young mother she was, about twenty-two or four, or along there; and blooming and lovely and sweet—oh, just a flower! And all her heart and all her soul was wrapped up in her child, her little girl, two years old. And it died, and she went wild with grief, just wild! Well, the only comfort she had was that she'd see her child again, in heaven—'never more to part,' she said, and kept on saying it over and over, 'never more to part.' And the words made her happy; yes, they did; they made her joyful; and when I was dying, twenty-seven years ago, she told me to find her child the first thing, and say she was coming—'soon, soon, *very* soon, she hoped and believed!' "
>
> "Why, it's pitiful, Sandy."
>
> He didn't say anything for a while, but sat looking at the ground, thinking. Then he says, kind of mournful:
>
> "And now she's come!"

Twain created this highly emotional situation for the two men as onlookers to real human grief. Twain was an honest enough writer to depict the grieving mother as middle-aged and desolate. Obviously Twain could never have published this passage if his wife had still been alive, with all the personal, familial references, including Livy's deep sorrows and her earlier thoughts about giving information to her father in "heaven."

Twain built upon this concept, creating and adding a touching segment about the aged woman looking for her child who had died in infancy. Sam Clemens's/ Mark Twain's life-experience enabled him to imagine sympathetically the developing rift between the mother, who remained about the same intellectually, and the child who developed somewhat precociously. The author, in his early seventies, knew how often the children outgrow their parents:

"Well, go on."

"Stormfield, maybe she hasn't found the child, but I think she has. Looks so to me. I've seen cases before. You see, she's kept that child in her head just the same as it was when she jounced it in her arms a little chubby thing. But it didn't elect to stay a child. No, it elected to grow up, which it did. And in these twenty-seven years it has learned all the deep scientific learning there is to learn, and is studying and studying and learning and learning more and more, all the time, and don't give a damn for anything but learning; just learning and learning, and discussing gigantic problems with people like herself."

"Well?"

"Stormfield, don't you see? Her mother knows *cranberries*, and how to tend them, and pick them and put them up, and market them; and not another blame thing! Her and her daughter can't be any more company for each other now than a mud-turtle and a bird of paradise. Poor thing, I think she's struck a disappointment."

"Sandy, what will they do?—stay unhappy forever in heaven?"

"No, they'll come together and get adjusted by and by. But not this year, and not next. By and by."

This seventy-three-year-old author wisely knew how children can grow to become distinct individuals, perhaps growing beyond or differently from what the parent had once expected or hoped for. Twain apparently also knew how beloved children can grow separate and apart, but ultimately have a reconciliation with parents.

Over the years Twain must have made many imaginative, creative, but difficult decisions about what to omit and what to keep and what to change. We may read some of this material with mixed emotions, including admiration for Twain's intellectual range, for his emotional empathy with the great variety of human situations. In a way, over the years the deaths of his family members may have gradually enabled Twain to express frankly complex, unconventional thoughts.

5. Targets

Twain used this book project as a magnet or collection point for a number of his satirical ideas about religion, societies, and cultures.

Twain's creative mind played with the location of "heaven" and with the speeds and directions of space travel; moreover, he also mocked the idea of having to load and transport fuel in order to resupply Satan's hellish fires. He also toyed with "necessary" but surprising topics, such as the climate in heaven and the cultural differences and nationalistic pride of the heavenly occupants. The mechanics of Twain's imagined "heaven" reveal that harps and wings are not really worth the trouble! Surprisingly, Twain's mind was imaginative and open enough to consider variations from humanoid creatures and cross-planetary cultural differences!

Certainly Twain was a relatively good hater. He nursed some angers, and he precisely focused his contempt to heap ridicule upon a Protestant minister, Thomas De Witt Talmage (1832–1902), who once headed a very large church in Brooklyn. In 1870 the man had earned a prominent place in Twain's personal contempt category, the author's own demonology. In that age, before frequent bathing and before antiperspirants, this Christian minister had stated:

> ...I have a good Christian friend who, if he sat in the front pew in church, and a working man should enter the door at the other end, would smell him instantly.... The fact is, if you had all the churches free, by reason of the mixing up of the common people with the uncommon, you would keep one-half of Christendom sick at their stomach. If you are going to kill the church thus with bad smells, I will have nothing to do with this work of evangelization.[11]

Twain took up his opposing argument because he felt deeply offended by Talmage's class bias. In a comically inconsistent way Twain certainly did not believe in "heaven," but he became very angry at Talmage for excluding working-class people. Twain probably realized that Talmage knew that "the common people" could not contribute as much as the wealthier members of the congregation might. How could a minister, supposedly an exemplar of Christian ethics, shamelessly exclude working-class people from the comforts and inclusion of a worshiping community? Twain's anger and scorn stayed sharply focused on Talmage, even nine years after his death.

Twain allowed for work, aging, and pain in his imagined "heaven," considering that a good part of "Happiness" depends on the contrast with what has gone before, depends upon the comparison with the previous activity. Twain applied some of what he had learned on Earth, putting limits on the privileges of the "elect" and imagining new forms of democratic "justice" in heaven, including giving great respect to ordinary, unknown, but significant people. For example, an unknown barkeeper and an unknown poet would have the highest privileges and honors in Twain's imagined but disbelieved "heaven." Moreover, he humanely imagined that people could keep developing in his "heaven." In a surprising demonstration of Twain's advanced, cosmopolitan cultural awareness, in Captain Stormfield's "heaven," Caucasians would be outnumbered by many generations of American Indians.

6. Conclusion

In November of 1909 the *New York Times Saturday Review of Books* gave first place on the American humor fall list to this book. The reviewer thought that Stormfield's "discoveries and experiences" would "make the orthodox gasp." The reviewer correctly analyzed that Twain used "the juxtaposition of incongruous ideas." And the reviewer concluded by judging that "there is an immense jot of philosophy of a shrewd and homely sort concerning the future life." People have passed copies on to friends, and the story has frequently been reprinted.

Nowadays many readers will enjoy reading this book for the satirical jabs at a conventional heaven. And many readers will also enjoy Twain's ability to create a comical tone, a strong narrator personality, a vivid description of unconventional scenes in heaven, and some amusing imagery. Twain cleverly ends his narrative by creating an allusive echo of a famous moment in his *Innocents Abroad*, when tourists scramble over and mark up the Egyptian Sphinx. Twain concludes with this metatextual comic remark about a planned heavenly monument, stating that "travellers would come for thousands of years and gawk at it, and climb over it, and scribble their names on it." Much of the fun in reading *Extract from Captain Stormfield's Visit to Heaven* comes from the author's literalist, logical humor about impossible beliefs. Twain, by taking literally many common beliefs about "heaven," makes us chuckle gently or laugh out loud. Knowledge of Twain's story will make it more difficult for us to hear ordinary, habitually repeated religious references without a grimace. In my judgment, Twain succeeds in mocking and undercutting the usually unquestioned, conventional, delusional concept of "heaven" that has been used to distract or placate suffering humanity and to compensate for, or promise postlife rewards for, global injustice.

I recommend that this book be read over at least two sittings. The book is best read calmly, perhaps with the comfort of a log-fire and a carafe of wine, with a notebook at hand to jot down ideas or phrases to bedevil a debating friend who has unthinkingly or carelessly grown to be an adult who still possesses, or is possessed by, childish ideas of "heaven."

The humane or considerate reader will realize, of course, that many friends could become angry or disoriented when their unquestioned notions of "heaven" are challenged. Many friends may feel chagrined when they realize that they have never really thought through such an impossibility. For many sincere, conventional persons the realization that their own previously unconsidered, childhood concepts are delusional may be shocking, disorienting, or difficult. For example, I would request that considerate debaters would politely delay or avoid debating with a person who has recently buried a child, such as the gifted singer Eric Clapton, whose son accidentally fell to his death. Clapton's musical creativity led him to write and sing a song to the child, "Will I See You in Heaven?" that demonstrates or reenacts this recurrent human tragedy.

I also recommend that both this book and Twain's *Letters from the Earth* are best read repeatedly, at approximately five-year intervals. As the reader continues to experience life, different parts of the *Visit to Heaven* will flash into sharper focus, will become clearer, more meaningful passages that convey Twain's wit and humanity. I suggest that Twain ultimately believed that this Earth is all we know of "heaven," and all we need to know of "hell."

Readers who wish to know more about this intriguing work may be advised to consult the superb editions of *Mark Twain's Notebooks and Journals,* published by the University of California Press and the fine edition of the *Twain-Howells Letters,* published by Harvard University Press. In addition, Frederik Pohl has written an interesting introduction and James A. Miller has contributed a fine afterword for *Extract from Captain Stormfield's Visit to Heaven* in the *Oxford Mark Twain Edition,* created by Shelley Fisher Fishkin. Readers who wish to read some more materials that Twain dropped from his *Extract* are advised to consult Dixon Wecter's 1952 *Report from Paradise* and Ray B. Browne's 1970 *Mark Twain's Quarrel with Heaven: "Captain Stormfield's Visit to Heaven" and Other Sketches.* And all readers of Twain are encouraged to support the Mark Twain Project at 480 Bancroft Library, University of California, Berkeley, CA, 94720-6000, under the leadership of Dr. Robert Hirst. This prize-winning research center will, when adequately funded, publish a complete, fully annotated edition of each of Twain's works, including whenever possible accurate texts of the manuscripts.

Victor Doyno
Professor of English
State University of New York at Buffalo
March 2002

NOTES

1. Mark Twain, "Memoranda," *Galaxy* 10, no. 4 (October 1870): 576.
2. Mark Twain, *Mark Twain's Notebooks and Journals*, ed. Frederick Anderson, Michael B. Frank, and Kenneth M. Sanderson, 3 vols. (Berkeley: University of California Press, 1975), 1:253.
3. Ibid., 1:247–48.
4. Ibid., 1:256–57.
5. Mark Twain, *Mark Twain-Howells Letters: The Correspondence of Samuel L. Clemens and William D. Howells, 1872–1910*, ed. Henry Nash Smith and William M. Gibson with Fred Anderson, 2 vols. (Cambridge, Mass.: Harvard University Press, Belknap Press, 1960), 2:661–62.
6. Ibid., 2:662–63.
7. Ibid., 2:785.
8. Ibid., 2:786.
9. Ibid., 2:787–88.
10. *Harper's Magazine.* The two installments of the early version can be found in vol. 116, no. 691 (December 1907): 41–49, and in vol. 116, no. 692 (January 1908): 266–76. The quotation appears on page 49.
11. Mark Twain, *Contributions to the Galaxy, 1868–1871,* ed. Bruce R. McElderry Jr. (Delmar, N.Y.: Scholars' Facsimiles & Reprints, 1977), 41. (Original publication occurred in the May 1870 *Galaxy*, page 721, "About Smells.")

Extract from Captain Stormfield's Visit to Heaven

ALBERT LEVERING

Extract from Captain Stormfield's Visit to Heaven

I

WELL, when I had been dead about thirty years, I begun to get a little anxious. Mind you, I had been whizzing through space all that time, like a comet. *Like* a comet! Why, Peters, I laid over the lot of them! Of course there warn't any of them going my way, as a steady thing, you know, because they travel in a long circle like the loop of a lasso, whereas I was pointed as straight as a dart for the Hereafter; but I happened on one every now and then that was going my way for an hour or so, and then we had a bit of a brush together. But it was generally pretty one-sided, because I sailed by them the same as if they were standing still. An ordinary comet don't make more than about 200,000 miles a minute. Of course when I came across one of that sort—like Encke's and Halley's comets, for instance—it warn't anything but just a flash and a vanish, you see. You couldn't rightly call it a race. It was as if the comet was a gravel-train and I was a telegraph despatch. But after I got outside of our astronomical system, I used to flush a comet occasionally that was something *like.* *We* haven't got any such comets — ours don't begin. One night I was swinging along at a good round gait, everything taut and trim, and the wind in my favor—I judged I was going about a million miles a minute—it might have been more, it couldn't have been less—when I flushed a most uncommonly big one about three points off my starboard bow. By his stern lights I judged he was bearing about northeast - and - by - north - half - east. Well, it was so near my course that I wouldn't throw away the chance; so I fell off a point, steadied my helm, and went for him. You should have heard me whiz, and seen the electric fur fly! In about a minute and a half I was fringed out with an electrical nimbus that flamed around for miles and miles and lit up all space like broad day. The comet was burning blue in the distance, like a sickly torch, when I first sighted him, but he begun to grow bigger and bigger as I crept up on him. I slipped up on him so fast that when I had gone about 150,000,000 miles I was close enough to be swallowed up in the phosphorescent glory of his wake, and I couldn't see anything for the glare. Thinks I, it won't do to run into him, so I shunted to one side and tore along. By and by I closed up abreast of his tail. Do you know what it was like? It was like a gnat closing up on the continent of America. I forged along. By and by I had sailed along his coast for a little upwards of a hundred and fifty million miles, and then I could see by the shape of him that I hadn't even got up to his waistband yet. Why, Peters, *we* don't know anything about comets, down here. If you want to see comets that *are* comets, you've got to go outside of our solar system—where there's room for them, you understand. My friend, I've seen comets out there that couldn't even lay down inside the *orbits* of our noblest comets without their tails hanging over.

Well, I boomed along another hundred and fifty million miles, and got up abreast his shoulder, as you may say. I was feeling pretty fine, I tell you; but just then I noticed the officer of the deck come to the side and hoist his glass in my direction. Straight off I heard him sing out—

"Below there, ahoy! Shake her up, shake her up! Heave on a hundred million billion tons of brimstone!"

"Ay—ay, sir!"

"Pipe the stabboard watch! All hands on deck!"

"Ay—ay, sir!"

"Send two hundred thousand million men aloft to shake out royals and sky-scrapers!"

"Ay—ay, sir!"

"Hand the stuns'ls! Hang out every rag you've got! Clothe her from stem to rudder-post!"

"Ay—ay, sir!"

In about a second I begun to see

I'd woke up a pretty ugly customer, Peters. In less than ten seconds that comet was just a blazing cloud of red-hot canvas. It was piled up into the heavens clean out of sight—the old thing seemed to swell out and occupy all space; the sulphur smoke from the furnaces—oh, well, nobody can describe the way it rolled and tumbled up into the skies, and nobody can half describe the way it smelt. Neither can anybody begin to describe the way that monstrous craft begun to crash along. And such another powwow — thousands of bo's'n's whistles screaming at once, and a crew like the populations of a hundred thousand worlds like ours all swearing at once. Well, I never heard the like of it before.

We roared and thundered along side by side, both doing our level best, because I'd never struck a comet before that could lay over me, and so I was bound to beat this one or break something. I judged I had some reputation in space, and I calculated to keep it. I noticed I wasn't gaining as fast, now, as I was before, but still I was gaining. There was a power of excitement on board the comet. Upwards of a hundred billion passengers swarmed up from below and rushed to the side and begun to bet on the race. Of course this careened her and damaged her speed. My, but wasn't the mate mad! He jumped at that crowd, with his trumpet in his hand, and sung out—

"Amidships! amidships, you ——![1] or I'll brain the last idiot of you!"

Well, sir, I gained and gained, little by little, till at last I went skimming sweetly by the magnificent old conflagration's nose. By this time the captain of the comet had been rousted out, and he stood there in the red glare for'ard, by the mate, in his shirt-sleeves and slippers, his hair all rats' nests and one suspender hanging, and how sick those two men did look! I just simply couldn't help putting my thumb to my nose as I glided away and singing out:

"Ta-ta! ta-ta! Any word to send to your family?"

Peters, it was a mistake. Yes, sir,

[1] The captain could not remember what this word was. He said it was in a foreign tongue.

I've often regretted that—it was a mistake. You see, the captain had given up the race, but that remark was too tedious for him—he couldn't stand it. He turned to the mate, and says he—

"Have we got brimstone enough of our own to make the trip?"

"Yes, sir."

"Sure?"

"Yes, sir—more than enough."

"How much have we got in cargo for Satan?"

"Eighteen hundred thousand billion quintillions of kazarks."

"Very well, then, let his boarders freeze till the next comet comes. Lighten ship! Lively, now, lively, men! Heave the whole cargo overboard!"

Peters, look me in the eye, and be calm. I found out, over there, that a kazark is exactly the bulk of a *hundred and sixty-nine worlds like ours!* They hove all that load overboard. When it fell it wiped out a considerable raft of stars just as clean as if they'd been candles and somebody blowed them out. As for the race, that was at an end. The minute she was lightened the comet swung along by me the same as if I was anchored. The captain stood on the stern, by the after-davits, and put his thumb to his nose and sung out—

"Ta-ta! ta-ta! Maybe *you've* got some message to send your friends in the Everlasting Tropics!"

Then he hove up his other suspender and started for'ard, and inside of three-quarters of an hour his craft was only a pale torch again in the distance. Yes, it was a mistake, Peters—that remark of mine. I don't reckon I'll ever get over being sorry about it. I'd 'a' beat the bully of the firmament if I'd kept my mouth shut.

But I've wandered a little off the track of my tale; I'll get back on my course again. Now you see what kind of speed I was making. So, as I said, when I had been tearing along this way about thirty years I begun to get uneasy. Oh, it was pleasant enough, with a good deal to find out, but then it was kind of lonesome, you know. Besides, I wanted to get somewhere.

I hadn't shipped with the idea of cruising forever. First off, I liked the delay, because I judged I was going to fetch up in pretty warm quarters when I got through; but towards the last I begun to feel that I'd rather go to — well, most any place, so as to finish up the uncertainty.

Well, one night—it was always night, except when I was rushing by some star that was occupying the whole universe with its fire and its glare—light enough then, of course, but I necessarily left it behind in a minute or two and plunged into a solid week of darkness again. The stars ain't so close together as they look to be. Where was I? Oh yes; one night I was sailing along, when I discovered a tremendous long row of blinking lights away on the horizon ahead. As I approached, they begun to tower and swell and look like mighty furnaces. Says I to myself—

"By George, I've arrived at last—and at the wrong place, just as I expected!"

Then I fainted. I don't know how long I was insensible, but it must have been a good while, for, when I came to, the darkness was all gone and there was the loveliest sunshine and the balmiest, fragrantest air in its place. And there was such a marvellous world spread out before me—such a glowing, beautiful, bewitching country. The things I took for furnaces were gates, miles high, made all of flashing jewels, and they pierced a wall of solid gold that you couldn't see the top of, nor yet the end of, in either direction. I was pointed straight for one of these gates, and a-coming like a house afire. Now I noticed that the skies were black with millions of people, pointed for those gates. What a roar they made, rushing through the air! The ground was as thick as ants with people, too—billions of them, I judge.

I lit. I drifted up to a gate with a swarm of people, and when it was my turn the head clerk says, in a business-like way—

"Well, quick! Where are you from?"

"San Francisco," says I.

"San Fran—*what?*" says he.

"San Francisco."

He scratched his head and looked puzzled, then he says—

"Is it a planet?"

By George, Peters, think of it! "*Planet?*" says I; "it's a city. And moreover, it's one of the biggest and finest and—"

"There, there!" says he, "no time here for conversation. We don't deal in cities here. Where are you from in a *general* way?"

"Oh," I says, "I beg your pardon. Put me down for California."

I had him *again*, Peters! He puzzled a second, then he says, sharp and irritable—

"I don't know any such planet—is it a constellation?"

"Oh, my goodness!" says I. "Constellation, says you? No—it's a State."

"Man, we don't deal in States here. *Will* you tell me where you are from *in general—at large*, don't you understand?"

"Oh, now I get your idea," I says. "I'm from America,—the United States of America."

Peters, do you know I had him *again?* If I hadn't I'm a clam! His face was as blank as a target after a militia shooting-match. He turned to an under clerk and says—

"Where is America? *What* is America?"

The under clerk answered up prompt and says—

"There ain't any such orb."

"*Orb?*" says I. "Why, what are

you talking about, young man? It ain't an orb; it's a country; it's a continent. Columbus discovered it; I reckon likely you've heard of *him*, anyway. America—why, sir, America—"

"Silence!" says the head clerk. "Once for all, where—are—you—*from?*"

"Well," says I, "I don't know anything more to say—unless I lump things, and just say I'm from the world."

"Ah," says he, brightening up, "now that's something like! *What* world?"

Peters, he had *me*, that time. I looked at him, puzzled, he looked at me, worried. Then he burst out—

"Come, come, what world?"

Says I, "Why, *the* world, of course."

"*The* world!" he says. "H'm! there's billions of them! . . . Next!"

That meant for me to stand aside. I done so, and a sky-blue man with seven heads and only one leg hopped into my place. I took a walk. It just occurred to me, then, that all the myriads I had seen swarming to that gate, up to this time, were just like that creature. I tried to run across somebody I was acquainted with, but they were out of acquaintances of mine just then. So I thought the thing all over and finally sidled back there pretty meek and feeling rather stumped, as you may say.

"Well?" said the head clerk.

"Well, sir," I says, pretty humble, "I don't seem to make out which world it is I'm from. But you may know it from this—it's the one the Saviour saved."

He bent his head at the Name. Then he says, gently—

"The worlds He has saved are like to the gates of heaven in number—none can count them. What astronomical system is your world in?—perhaps that may assist."

"It's the one that has the sun in it—and the moon—and Mars"—he shook his head at each name—hadn't ever heard of them, you see—"and Neptune—and Uranus—and Jupiter—"

"Hold on!" says he—"hold on a minute! Jupiter . . . Jupiter . . . Seems to me we had a man from there eight or nine hundred years ago—but people from that system very seldom enter by this gate." All of a sudden he begun to look me so straight in the eye that I thought he was going to bore through me. Then he says, very deliberate, "Did you come *straight here* from your system?"

"Yes, sir," I says—but I blushed the least little bit in the world when I said it.

He looked at me very stern, and says—

"That is not true; and this is not the place for prevarication. You wandered from your course. How did that happen?"

Says I, blushing again—

"I'm sorry, and I take back what I said, and confess. I raced a little with a comet one day—only just the least little bit—only the tiniest lit—"

"So—so," says he—and without any sugar in his voice to speak of.

I went on, and says—

"But I only fell off just a bare point, and I went right back on my course again the minute the race was over."

"No matter—that divergence has made all this trouble. It has brought you to a gate that is billions of leagues from the right one. If you had gone to your own gate they would have known all about your world at once and there would have been no delay. But we will try to accommodate you." He turned to an under clerk and says—

"What system is Jupiter in?"

"I don't remember, sir, but I think there is such a planet in one of the little new systems away out in one of the thinly worlded corners of the universe. I will see."

He got a balloon and sailed up and up and up, in front of a map that was as big as Rhode Island. He went on up till he was out of sight, and by and by he came down and got something to eat and went up again. To cut a long story short, he kept on doing this for a day or two, and finally he came down and said he thought he had found that solar system, but it might be fly-specks. So he got a microscope and went back. It turned out better than he feared. He had rousted out our system, sure enough. He got me to describe our planet and its distance from the sun, and then he says to his chief—

"Oh, I know the one he means, now, sir. It is on the map. It is called the Wart."

Says I to myself, "Young man, it wouldn't be wholesome for you to go down *there* and call it the Wart."

Well, they let me in, then, and told me I was safe forever and wouldn't have any more trouble.

Then they turned from me and went on with their work, the same as if they considered my case all complete and shipshape. I was a good deal surprised at this, but I was diffident about speaking up and reminding them. I did so hate to do it, you know; it seemed a pity to bother them, they had so much on their hands. Twice I thought I would give up and let the thing go; so twice I started to leave, but immediately I thought what a figure I should cut stepping out amongst the redeemed in such a rig, and that made me hang back and come to anchor again. People got to eying me—clerks, you know—wondering why I didn't get under way. I couldn't stand this long—it was too uncomfortable. So at last I plucked up courage and tipped the head clerk a signal. He says—

"What! you here yet? What's wanting?"

Says I, in a low voice and very confidential, making a trumpet with my hands at his ear—

"I beg pardon, and you mustn't

mind my reminding you, and seeming to meddle, but hain't you forgot something?"

He studied a second, and says—

"Forgot something? . . . No, not that I know of."

"Think," says I.

He thought. Then he says—

"No, I can't seem to have forgot anything. What is it?"

"Look at me," says I, "look me all over."

He done it.

"Well?" says he.

"Well," says I, "you don't notice anything? If I branched out amongst the elect looking like this, wouldn't I attract considerable attention?—wouldn't I be a little conspicuous?"

"Well," he says, "I don't see anything the matter. What do you lack?"

"Lack! Why, I lack my harp, and my wreath, and my halo, and my hymn-book, and my palm branch—I lack everything that a body naturally requires up here, my friend."

Puzzled? Peters, he was the worst puzzled man you ever saw. Finally he says—

"Well, you seem to be a curiosity every way a body takes you. I never heard of these things before."

I looked at the man awhile in solid astonishment; then I says—

"Now, I hope you don't take it as an offence, for I don't mean any, but really, for a man that has been in the Kingdom as long as I reckon you have, you do seem to know powerful little about its customs."

"Its customs!" says he. "Heaven is a large place, good friend. Large empires have many and diverse customs. Even small dominions have, as you doubtless know by what you have seen of the matter on a small scale in the Wart. How can you imagine I could ever learn the varied customs of the countless kingdoms of heaven? It makes my head ache to think of it. I know the customs that prevail in those portions inhabited by peoples that are appointed to enter by my own gate—and hark ye, that is quite enough knowledge for one individual to try to pack into his head in the thirty-seven millions of years I have devoted night and day to that study. But the idea of learning the customs of the whole appalling expanse of heaven—O man, how insanely you talk! Now I don't doubt that this odd costume you talk about is the fashion in that district of heaven you belong to, but you won't be conspicuous in this section without it."

I felt all right, if that was the case, so I bade him good-day and left. All day I walked towards the far end of a prodigious hall of the office, hoping to come out into heaven any moment, but it was a mistake. That hall was built on the general heavenly plan—it naturally couldn't be small. At last I got so tired I couldn't go any farther; so I sat down to rest, and begun to tackle the queerest sort of strangers and ask for information;

but I didn't get any; they couldn't understand my language, and I could not understand theirs. I got dreadfully lonesome. I was so downhearted and homesick I wished a hundred times I never had died. I turned back, of course. About noon next day, I got back at last and was on hand at the booking-office once more. Says I to the head clerk—

"I begin to see that a man's got to be in his own heaven to be happy."

"Perfectly correct," says he. "Did you imagine the same heaven would suit all sorts of men?"

"Well, I had that idea—but I see the foolishness of it. Which way am I to go to get to my district?"

He called the under clerk that had examined the map, and he gave me general directions. I thanked him and started; but he says—

"Wait a minute; it is millions of leagues from here. Go outside and stand on that red wishing-carpet; shut your eyes, hold your breath, and wish yourself there."

"I'm much obliged," says I; "why didn't you dart me through when I first arrived?"

"We have a good deal to think of here; it was your place to think of it and ask for it. Good-by; we probably sha'n't see you in this region for a thousand centuries or so."

"In that case, *o revoor*," says I.

I hopped onto the carpet and held my breath and shut my eyes and wished I was in the booking-office of my own section. The very next instant a voice I knew sung out in a business kind of a way—

"A harp and a hymn-book, pair of wings and a halo, size 13, for Cap'n Eli Stormfield, of San Francisco!—make him out a clean bill of health, and let him in."

I opened my eyes. Sure enough, it was a Pi Ute Injun I used to know in Tulare County; mighty good fellow—I remembered being at his funeral, which consisted of him being burnt and the other Injuns gauming their faces with his ashes and howling like wildcats. He was powerful glad to see me, and you may make up your mind I was just as glad to see him, and feel that I was in the right kind of a heaven at last.

Just as far as your eye could reach,

there was swarms of clerks, running and bustling around, tricking out thousands of Yanks and Mexicans and English and A-rabs, and all sorts of people in their new outfits; and when they gave me my kit and I put on my halo and took a look in the glass, I could have jumped over a house for joy, I was so happy. "Now *this* is something like!" says I. "Now," says I, "I'm all right—show me a cloud."

Inside of fifteen minutes I was a mile on my way towards the cloud-banks and about a million people along with me. Most of us tried to fly, but some got crippled and nobody made a success of it. So we concluded to walk, for the present, till we had had some wing practice.

We begun to meet swarms of folks who were coming back. Some had harps and nothing else; some had hymn-books and nothing else; some had nothing at all; all of them looked meek and uncomfortable; one young fellow hadn't anything left but his halo, and he was carrying that in his hand; all of a sudden he offered it to me and says—

"Will you hold it for me a minute?"

Then he disappeared in the crowd. I went on. A woman asked me to hold her palm branch, and then *she* disappeared. A girl got me to hold her harp for her, and by George, *she* disappeared; and so on and so on, till I was about loaded down to the guards. Then comes a smiling old gentleman and asked me to hold *his* things. I swabbed off the perspiration and says, pretty tart—

"I'll have to get you to excuse me, my friend,—*I* ain't no hat-rack."

About this time I begun to run across piles of those traps, lying in the road. I just quietly dumped my extra cargo along with them. I looked around, and, Peters, that whole nation that was following me were loaded down the same as I'd been. The return crowd had got them to hold their things a minute, you see. They all dumped their loads, too, and we went on.

When I found myself perched on a cloud, with a million other people, I never felt so good in my life. Says I, "Now this is according to the promises; I've been having my doubts, but now I *am* in heaven, sure enough." I gave my palm branch a wave or two, for luck, and then I tautened up my harp-strings and struck in. Well, Peters, you can't imagine anything like the row we made. It was grand to listen to, and made a body thrill all over, but there was considerable many tunes going on at once, and that was a drawback to the harmony, you understand; and then there was a lot of Injun tribes, and they kept up such another war-whooping that they kind of took the tuck out of the music. By and by I quit performing, and judged I'd take a rest. There was quite a nice mild old gentleman sitting next me, and I noticed he didn't take a hand; I encouraged him, but he said he was naturally bashful, and was afraid to try before so many people. By and by the old gentleman said he never could seem to enjoy music somehow. The fact was, I was beginning to feel the same way; but I didn't say anything. Him and I had a considerable long silence, then, but of course it warn't noticeable in that place. After about sixteen or seventeen hours, during which I played and sung a little, now and then—always the same tune, because I didn't know any other—I laid down my harp and begun to fan myself with my palm branch. Then we both got to sighing pretty regular. Finally, says he—

"Don't you know any tune but the one you've been pegging at all day?"

"Not another blessed one," says I.

"Don't you reckon you could learn another one?" says he.

"Never," says I; "I've tried to, but I couldn't manage it."

"It's a long time to hang to the one—eternity, you know."

"Don't break my heart," says I; "I'm getting low-spirited enough already."

After another long silence, says he—

"Are you glad to be here?"

Says I, "Old man, I'll be frank with you. This *ain't* just as near my idea of bliss as I thought it was going to be, when I used to go to church."

Says he, "What do you say to knocking off and calling it half a day?"

"That's me," says I. "I never

wanted to get off watch so bad in my life."

So we started. Millions were coming to the cloud-bank all the time, happy and hosannahing; millions were leaving it all the time, looking mighty quiet, I tell you. We laid for the new-comers, and pretty soon I'd got them to hold all my things a minute, and then I was a free man again and most outrageously happy. Just then I ran across old Sam Bartlett, who had been dead a long time, and stopped to have a talk with him. Says I—

"Now tell me—is this to go on forever? Ain't there anything else for a change?"

Says he—

"I'll set you right on that point

very quick. People take the figurative language of the Bible and the allegories for literal, and the first thing they ask for when they get here is a halo and a harp, and so on. Nothing that's harmless and reasonable is refused a body here, if he asks it in the right spirit. So they are outfitted with these things without a word. They go and sing and play just about one day, and that's the last you'll ever see them in the choir. They don't need anybody to tell them that that sort of thing wouldn't make a heaven—at least not a heaven that a sane man could stand a week and remain sane. That cloud-bank is placed where the noise can't disturb the old inhabitants, and so there ain't any harm in letting everybody get up there and cure himself as soon as he comes.

"Now you just remember this—heaven is as blissful and lovely as it can be; but it's just the busiest place you ever heard of. There ain't any idle people here after the first day. Singing hymns and waving palm branches through all eternity is pretty when you hear about it in the pulpit, but it's as poor a way to put in valuable time as a body could contrive. It would just make a heaven of warbling ignoramuses, don't you see? Eternal Rest sounds comforting in the pulpit, too. Well, you try it once, and see how heavy time will hang on your hands. Why, Stormfield, a man like you, that had been active and stirring all his life, would go mad in six months in a heaven where he hadn't anything to do. Heaven is the very last place to come to *rest* in,—and don't you be afraid to bet on that!"

Says I—

"Sam, I'm as glad to hear it as I thought I'd be sorry. I'm glad I come, now."

Says he—

"Cap'n, ain't you pretty physically tired?"

Says I—

"Sam, it ain't any name for it! I'm dog-tired."

"Just so—just so. You've earned a good sleep, and you'll get it. You've earned a good appetite, and you'll enjoy your dinner. It's the same here as it is on earth—you've got to earn a thing, square and honest, before you enjoy it. You can't enjoy first and earn afterwards. But there's this difference, here: you can choose your own occupation, and all the powers of heaven will be put forth to help you make a success of it, if you do your level best. The shoemaker on earth that had the soul of a poet in him won't have to make shoes here."

"Now that's all reasonable and right," says I. "Plenty of work, and the kind you hanker after; no more pain, no more suffering—"

"Oh, hold on; there's plenty of pain here—but it don't kill. There's plenty of suffering here, but it don't last. You see, happiness ain't a *thing in itself* — it's only a *contrast* with something that ain't pleasant. That's all it is. There ain't a thing you can mention that is happiness in its own self—it's only so by contrast with the other thing. And so, as soon as the novelty is over and the force of the contrast dulled, it ain't happiness any longer, and you have to get something fresh. Well, there's plenty of pain and suffering in heaven—consequently there's plenty of contrasts, and just no end of happiness."

Says I, "It's the sensiblest heaven I've heard of yet, Sam, though it's about as different from the one I was brought up on as a live princess is different from her own wax figger."

Along in the first months I knocked around about the Kingdom, making friends and looking at the country, and finally settled down in a pretty likely region, to have a rest before taking another start. I went on making acquaintances and gathering up information. I had a good deal of talk with an old bald-headed angel by the name of Sandy McWilliams. He was from somewhere in New Jersey. I went about with him, considerable. We used to lay around, warm afternoons, in the shade of a rock, on some meadow-ground that was pretty high and out of the marshy slush of his cranberry-farm, and there we used to talk about all kinds of things, and smoke pipes. One day, says I—

"About how old might you be, Sandy?"

"Seventy-two."

"I judged so. How long you been in heaven?"

"Twenty-seven years, come Christmas."

"How old was you when you come up?"

"Why, seventy-two, of course."

"You can't mean it!"

"Why can't I mean it?"

"Because, if you was seventy-two then, you are naturally ninety-nine now."

"No, but I ain't. I stay the same age I was when I come."

"Well," says I, "come to think, there's something just here that I want to ask about. Down below, I always had an idea that in heaven we would all be young, and bright, and spry."

"Well, you *can* be young if you want to. You've only got to wish."

"Well, then, why didn't you wish?"

"I did. They all do. You'll try it, some day, like enough; but you'll get tired of the change pretty soon."

"Why?"

"Well, I'll tell you. Now you've always been a sailor; did you ever try some other business?"

"Yes, I tried keeping grocery, once, up in the mines; but I couldn't stand it; it was too dull—no stir, no storm, no life about it; it was like being part dead and part alive, both at the same time. I wanted to be one thing or t'other. I shut up shop pretty quick and went to sea."

"That's it. Grocery people like it, but you couldn't. You see you wasn't used to it. Well, I wasn't used to being young, and I couldn't seem to take any interest in it. I was strong, and handsome, and had curly hair, —yes, and wings, too!—gay wings like a butterfly. I went to picnics and dances and parties with the fellows, and tried to carry on and talk nonsense with the girls, but it wasn't any use; I couldn't take to it—fact is, it was an awful bore. What I wanted was early to bed and early to rise, and something to *do;* and when my work was done, I wanted to sit quiet, and smoke and think—not tear around with a parcel of giddy young kids. You can't think what I suffered whilst I was young."

"How long was you young?"

"Only two weeks. That was plenty

for me. Laws, I was so lonesome! You see, I was full of the knowledge and experience of seventy-two years; the deepest subject those young folks could strike was only *a-b-c* to me. And to hear them argue—oh, my! it would have been funny, if it hadn't been so pitiful. Well, I was so hungry for the ways and the sober talk I was used to, that I tried to ring in with the old people, but they wouldn't have it. They considered me a conceited young upstart, and gave me the cold shoulder. Two weeks was a-plenty for me. I was glad to get back my bald head again, and my pipe, and my old drowsy reflections in the shade of a rock or a tree."

"Well," says I, "do you mean to

say you're going to stand still at seventy-two, forever?"

"I don't know, and I ain't particular. But I ain't going to drop back to twenty-five any more—I know that, mighty well. I know a sight more than I did twenty-seven years ago, and I enjoy learning, all the time, but I don't seem to get any older. That is, bodily—my mind gets older, and stronger, and better seasoned, and more satisfactory."

Says I, "If a man comes here at ninety, don't he ever set himself back?"

"Of course he does. He sets himself back to fourteen; tries it a couple of hours, and feels like a fool; sets himself forward to twenty; it ain't much improvement; tries thirty, fifty, eighty, and finally ninety—finds he is more at home and comfortable at the same old figure he is used to than any other way. Or, if his mind begun to fail him on earth at eighty, that's where he finally sticks up here. He sticks at the place where his mind was last at its best, for there's where his enjoyment is best, and his ways most set and established."

"Does a chap of twenty-five stay always twenty-five, and look it?"

"If he is a fool, yes. But if he is bright, and ambitious and industrious, the knowledge he gains and the experiences he has, change his ways and thoughts and likings, and make him find his best pleasure in the company of people above that age; so he allows his body to take on that look of as many added years as he needs to make him comfortable and proper in that sort of society; he lets his body go on taking the look of age, according as he progresses, and by and by he will be bald and wrinkled outside, and wise and deep within."

"Babies the same?"

"Babies the same. Laws, what asses we used to be, on earth, about these things! We said we'd be always young in heaven. We didn't say *how* young—we didn't think of that, perhaps—that is, we didn't all think alike, anyway. When I was a boy of seven, I suppose I thought we'd all be twelve, in heaven; when I was twelve, I suppose I thought we'd all be eighteen or twenty in heaven; when I was forty, I begun to go back;

I remember I hoped we'd all be about *thirty* years old in heaven. Neither a man nor a boy ever thinks the age he *has* is exactly the best one—he puts the *right* age a few years older or a few years younger than he is. Then he makes that ideal age the general age of the heavenly people. And he expects everybody *to stick* at that age—stand stock-still—and expects them to enjoy it!—Now just think of the idea of standing still in heaven! Think of a heaven made up entirely of hoop-rolling, marble-playing cubs of seven years!—or of awkward, diffident, sentimental immaturities of nineteen!—or of vigorous people of thirty, healthy-minded, brimming with ambition, but chained hand and foot to that one age and its limitations like so many helpless galley-slaves! Think of the dull sameness of a society made up of people all of one age and one set of looks, habits, tastes and feelings. Think how superior to it earth would be, with its variety of types and faces and ages, and the enlivening attrition of the myriad interests that come into pleasant collision in such a variegated society."

"Look here," says I, "do you know what you're doing?"

"Well, what am I doing?"

"You are making heaven pretty comfortable in one way, but you are playing the mischief with it in another."

"How d'you mean?"

"Well," I says, "take a young mother that's lost her child, and—"

"'Sh!" he says. "Look!"

It was a woman. Middle-aged, and had grizzled hair. She was walking slow, and her head was bent down, and her wings hanging limp and droopy; and she looked ever so tired, and was crying, poor thing! She passed along by, with her head down, that way, and the tears running down her face, and didn't see us. Then Sandy said, low and gentle, and full of pity:

"*She's* hunting for her child! No, *found* it, I reckon. Lord, how she's changed! But I recognized her in a minute, though it's twenty-seven years since I saw her. A young mother she was, about twenty two or four, or along there; and blooming and lovely and sweet? oh, just a flower! And all her heart and all her soul was wrapped up in her child, her little girl, two years old. And it died, and she went wild with grief, just wild! Well, the only comfort she had was that she'd see her child again, in heaven—'never more to part,' she said, and kept on saying it over and over, 'never more to part.' And the words made her happy; yes, they did; they made her joyful; and when I was dying, twenty-seven years ago, she told me to find her child the first thing, and say she was coming—'soon, soon, *very* soon, she hoped and believed!'"

"Why, it's pitiful, Sandy."

He didn't say anything for a while, but sat looking at the ground, thinking. Then he says, kind of mournful:

"And now she's come!"

"Well? Go on."

"Stormfield, maybe she hasn't found the child, but *I* think she has. Looks so to me. I've seen cases before. You see, she's kept that child in her head just the same as it was when she jounced it in her arms a little chubby thing. But here it didn't elect to *stay* a child. No, it elected to grow up, which it did. And in these twenty-seven years it has learned all the deep scientific learning there is to learn, and is studying and studying and learning and learning more and more, all the time, and don't give a damn for anything *but* learning; just learning, and discussing gigantic problems with people like herself."

"Well?"

"Stormfield, don't you see? Her mother knows *cranberries*, and how to tend them, and pick them, and put them up, and market them; and not another blamed thing! Her and her daughter can't be any more company for each other *now* than mud turtle and bird o' paradise. Poor thing, she was looking for a baby to jounce; *I* think she's struck a disapp'intment."

"Sandy, what will they do—stay unhappy forever in heaven?"

"No, they'll come together and get adjusted by and by. But not this year, and not next. By and by."

II

I HAD been having considerable trouble with my wings. The day after I helped the choir I made a dash or two with them, but was not lucky. First off, I flew thirty yards, and then fouled an Irishman and brought him down—brought us both down, in fact. Next, I had a collision with a Bishop—and bowled him down, of course. We had some sharp words, and I felt pretty cheap, to come banging into a grave old person like that, with a million strangers looking on and smiling to themselves.

I saw I hadn't got the hang of the steering, and so couldn't rightly tell where I was going to bring up when I started. I went afoot the rest of the day, and let my wings hang. Early next morning I went to a private place to have some practice. I got up on a pretty high rock, and got a good start, and went swooping down, aiming for a bush a little over three hundred yards off; but I couldn't seem to calculate for the wind, which was about two points abaft my beam. I could see I was going considerable to looard of the bush, so I worked my starboard wing slow and went ahead strong on the port one, but it wouldn't answer; I could see I was going to broach to, so I slowed down on both, and lit. I went back to the rock and took another chance at it. I aimed two or three points to starboard of the bush—yes, more than that—enough so as to make it nearly a head-wind. I done well enough, but made pretty poor time. I could see, plain enough, that on a head-wind, wings was a mistake. I could see that a body could sail pretty close to the wind, but he couldn't go in the wind's eye. I could see that if I wanted to go a-visiting any distance from home, and the wind was ahead, I might have to wait days, maybe, for a change; and I could see, too, that these things could not be any use at all in a gale; if you tried to run before the wind, you would make a mess of it, for there isn't any way to shorten sail—like reefing, you know—you have to take it *all* in—shut your feathers down flat to your sides. That would *land* you, of course. You could lay to, with your head to the wind—that is the best you could do, and right hard work you'd find it, too. If you tried any other game, you would founder, sure.

I judge it was about a couple of weeks or so after this that I dropped old Sandy McWilliams a note one day—it was a Tuesday—and asked him to come over and take his manna and quails with me next day; and the first thing he did when he stepped in was to twinkle his eye in a sly way, and say,—

"Well, Cap, what you done with your wings?"

I saw in a minute that there was some sarcasm done up in that rag somewheres, but I never let on. I only says,—

"Gone to the wash."

"Yes," he says, in a dry sort of way, "they mostly go to the wash—about this time—I've often noticed it. Fresh angels are powerful neat. When do you look for 'em back?"

"Day after to-morrow," says I.

He winked at me, and smiled.

Says I,—

"Sandy, out with it. Come—no secrets among friends. I notice you don't ever wear wings—and plenty others don't. I've been making an ass of myself—is that it?"

"That is about the size of it. But it is no harm. We all do it at first.

It's perfectly natural. You see, on earth we jump to such foolish conclusions as to things up here. In the pictures we always saw the angels with wings on—and that was all right; but we jumped to the conclusion that that was their way of getting around—and that was all wrong. The wings ain't anything but a uniform, that's all. When they are in the field—so to speak,—they always wear them; you never see an angel going with a message anywhere without his wings, any more than you would see a military officer presiding at a court-martial without his uniform, or a postman delivering letters, or a policeman walking his beat, in plain clothes. But they ain't to *fly* with! The wings are for show, not for use. Old experienced angels are like officers of the regular army — they dress plain, when they are off duty. New angels are like the militia—never shed the uniform — always fluttering and floundering around in their wings, butting people down, flapping here, and there, and everywhere, always imagining they are attracting the admiring eye—well, they just think they are the very most important people in heaven. And when you see one of them come sailing around with one wing tipped up and t'other down, you make up your mind he is saying to himself: 'I wish Mary Ann in Arkansaw could see me now. I reckon she'd wish she hadn't shook me.' No, they're just for show, that's all—only just for show."

"I judge you've got it about right, Sandy," says I.

"Why, look at it yourself," says he. "*You* ain't built for wings—no man is. You know what a grist of years it took you to come here from the earth—and yet you were booming along faster than any cannon-ball could go. Suppose you had to fly that distance with your wings—wouldn't eternity have been over before you got here? Certainly. Well, angels have to go to the earth every day—millions of them—to appear in visions to dying children and good people, you know—it's the heft of their business. They appear with their wings, of course, because they are on official service, and because the dying persons wouldn't know they were angels if they hadn't wings—but do you reckon they fly with them? It stands to reason they don't. The wings would wear out before they got half-way; even the pin-feathers would be gone; the wing frames would be as bare as kite sticks before the paper is pasted on. The distances in heaven are billions of times greater; angels have to go all over heaven every day; could they do it with their wings alone? No, indeed; they wear the wings for style, but they travel any distance in an instant by *wishing*. The wishing-carpet of the Arabian Nights was a sensible idea—but our earthly idea of angels flying these awful distances with their clumsy wings was foolish.

"Our young saints, of both sexes,

wear wings all the time—blazing red ones, and blue and green, and gold, and variegated, and rainbowed, and ring-streaked-and-striped ones—and nobody finds fault. It is suitable to their time of life. The things are beautiful, and they set the young people off. They are the most striking and lovely part of their outfit—a halo don't *begin*."

"Well," says I, "I've tucked mine away in the cupboard, and I allow to let them lay there till there's mud."

"Yes—or a reception."

"What's that?"

"Well, you can see one to-night if you want to. There's a barkeeper from Jersey City going to be received."

"Go on—tell me about it."

"This barkeeper got converted at a Moody and Sankey meeting, in New York, and started home on the ferry-boat, and there was a collision and he got drowned. He is of a class that think all heaven goes wild with joy when a particularly hard lot like him is saved; they think all heaven turns out hosannahing to welcome them; they think there isn't anything talked about in the realms of the blest but their case, for that day. This bar-keeper thinks there hasn't been such another stir here in years, as his coming is going to raise.—And I've always noticed this peculiarity about a dead barkeeper—he not only expects all hands to turn out when he arrives, but he expects to be received with a torchlight procession."

"I reckon he is disappointed, then."

"No, he isn't. No man is allowed to be disappointed here. Whatever he wants, when he comes—that is, any reasonable and unsacrilegious thing—he can have. There's always a few millions or billions of young folks around who don't want any better entertainment than to fill up their lungs and swarm out with their torches and have a high time over a barkeeper. It tickles the barkeeper till he can't rest, it makes a charming lark for the young folks, it don't do anybody any harm, it don't cost a rap, and it keeps up the place's reputation for making all comers happy and content."

"Very good. I'll be on hand and see them land the barkeeper."

"It is manners to go in full dress. You want to wear your wings, you know, and your other things."

"Which ones?"

"Halo, and harp, and palm branch, and all that."

"Well," says I, "I reckon I ought to be ashamed of myself, but the fact is I left them laying around that day I resigned from the choir. I haven't got a rag to wear but this robe and the wings."

"That's all right. You'll find they've been raked up and saved for you. Send for them."

"I'll do it, Sandy. But what was it you was saying about unsacrilegious things, which people expect to get, and will be disappointed about?"

"Oh, there are a lot of such things

that people expect and don't get. For instance, there's a Brooklyn preacher by the name of Talmage, who is laying up a considerable disappointment for himself. He says, every now and then in his sermons, that the first thing he does when he gets to heaven, will be to fling his arms around Abraham, Isaac and Jacob, and kiss them and weep on them. There's millions of people down there on earth that are promising themselves the same thing. As many as sixty thousand people arrive here every single day, that want to run straight to Abraham, Isaac and Jacob, and hug them and weep on them. Now mind you, sixty thousand a day is a pretty heavy contract for those old people. If they were a mind to allow it, they wouldn't ever have anything to do, year in and year out, but stand up and be hugged and wept on thirty-two hours in the twenty-four. They would be tired out and as wet as muskrats all the time. What would heaven be, to *them?* It would be a mighty good place to get out of—you know that, yourself. Those are kind and gentle old Jews, but they ain't any fonder of kissing the emotional highlights of Brooklyn than you be. You mark my words, Mr. T.'s endearments are going to be declined, with thanks. There are limits to the privileges of the elect, even in heaven. Why, if Adam was to show himself to every new comer that wants to call and gaze at him and strike him for his autograph, he would never have time to do anything else but just that. Talmage has said he is going to give Adam some of his attentions, as well as A., I. and J. But he will have to change his mind about that."

"Do you think Talmage will really come here?"

"Why, certainly, he will; but don't you be alarmed; he will run with his own kind, and there's plenty of them. That is the main charm of heaven—there's all kinds here—which wouldn't be the case if you let the preachers tell it. Anybody can find the sort he prefers, here, and he just lets the others alone, and they let him alone. When the Deity builds a heaven, it is built right, and on a liberal plan."

Sandy sent home for his things, and I sent for mine, and about nine in the evening we begun to dress. Sandy says,—

"This is going to be a grand time for you, Stormy. Like as not some of the patriarchs will turn out."

"No, but will they?"

"Like as not. Of course they are pretty exclusive. They hardly ever show themselves to the common public. I believe they never turn out except for an eleventh-hour convert. They wouldn't do it then, only earthly tradition makes a grand show pretty necessary on that kind of an occasion."

"Do they all turn out, Sandy?"

"Who?—all the patriarchs? Oh, no—hardly ever more than a couple.

You will be here fifty thousand years —maybe more—before you get a glimpse of all the patriarchs and prophets. Since I have been here, Job has been to the front once, and once Ham and Jeremiah both at the same time. But the finest thing that has happened in my day was a year or so ago; that was Charles Peace's reception—him they called 'the Bannercross Murderer'—an Englishman. There were four patriarchs and two prophets on the Grand Stand that time — there hasn't been anything like it since Captain Kidd came; Abel was there — the first time in twelve hundred years. A report got around that Adam was coming; well, of course, Abel was enough to bring a crowd, all by himself, but there is nobody that can draw like Adam. It was a false report, but it got around, anyway, as I say, and it will be a long day before I see the like of it again. The reception was in the English department, of course, which is eight hundred and eleven million miles from the New Jersey line. I went, along with a good many of my neighbors, and it was a sight to see, I can tell you. Flocks came from all the departments. I saw Esquimaux there, and Tartars, negroes, Chinamen—people from everywhere. You see a mixture like that in the Grand Choir, the first day you land here, but you hardly ever see it again. There were billions of people; when they were singing or hosannahing, the noise was wonderful; and even when their tongues were still the drumming of the wings was nearly enough to burst your head, for all the sky was as thick as if it was snowing angels. Although Adam was not there, it was a great time anyway, because we had three archangels on the Grand Stand—it is a seldom thing that even one comes out."

"What did they look like, Sandy?"

"Well, they had shining faces, and shining robes, and wonderful rainbow wings, and they stood eighteen feet high, and wore swords, and held their heads up in a noble way, and looked like soldiers."

"Did they have halos?"

"No—anyway, not the hoop kind. The archangels and the upper-class patriarchs wear a finer thing than that. It is a round, solid, splendid glory of gold, that is blinding to look at. You have often seen a patriarch in a picture, on earth, with that thing on—you remember it?—he looks as if he had his head in a brass platter. That don't give you the right idea of it at all—it is much more shining and beautiful."

"Did you talk with those archangels and patriarchs, Sandy?"

"Who—*I?* Why, what can you be thinking about, Stormy? I ain't worthy to speak to such as they."

"Is Talmage?"

"Of course not. You have got the same mixed-up idea about these things that everybody has down there. I had it once, but I got over it. Down there they talk of the heavenly King—and that is right—

but then they go right on speaking as if this was a republic and everybody was on a dead level with everybody else, and privileged to fling his arms around anybody he comes across, and be hail-fellow-well-met with all the elect, from the highest down. How tangled up and absurd that is! How are you going to have a republic under a king? How are you going to have a republic at all, where the head of the government is absolute, holds his place forever, and has no parliament, no council to meddle or make in his affairs, nobody voted for, nobody elected, nobody in the whole universe with a voice in the government, nobody asked to take a hand in its matters, and nobody *allowed* to do it? Fine republic, ain't it?"

"Well, yes—it *is* a little different from the idea I had—but I thought I might go around and get acquainted with the grandees, anyway—not exactly splice the main-brace with them, you know, but shake hands and pass the time of day."

"Could Tom, Dick and Harry call on the Cabinet of Russia and do that? — on Prince Gortschakoff, for instance?"

"I reckon not, Sandy."

"Well, this is Russia—only more so. There's not the shadow of a republic about it anywhere. There are ranks, here. There are viceroys, princes, governors, sub-governors, sub-sub-governors, and a hundred orders of nobility, grading along down from grand-ducal archangels, stage by stage, till the general level is struck, where there ain't any titles. Do you know what a prince of the blood is, on earth?"

"No."

"Well, a prince of the blood don't belong to the royal family exactly, and he don't belong to the mere nobility of the kingdom; he is lower than the one, and higher than t'other. That's about the position of the patriarchs and prophets here. There's some mighty high nobility here—people that you and I ain't worthy to polish sandals for—and *they* ain't worthy to polish sandals for the patriarchs and prophets. That gives you a kind of an idea of their rank, don't it? You begin to see how high up they are, don't you? Just to get a two-minute glimpse of one of them is a thing for a body to remember and tell about for a thousand years. Why, Captain, just think of this: if Abraham was to set his foot down here by this door, there would be a railing set up around that foot-track right away, and a shelter put over it, and people would flock here from all over heaven, for hundreds and hundreds of years, to look at it. Abraham is one of the parties that Mr. Talmage, of Brooklyn, is going to embrace, and kiss, and weep on, when he comes. He wants to lay in a good stock of tears, you know, or five to one he will go dry before he gets a chance to do it."

"Sandy," says I, "I had an idea that *I* was going to be equals with everybody here, too, but I will let that drop. It don't matter, and I am plenty happy enough anyway."

"Captain, you are happier than you would be, the other way. These old patriarchs and prophets have got ages the start of you; they know more in two minutes than you know in a year. Did you ever try to have a sociable improving-time discussing winds, and currents and variations of compass with an undertaker?"

"I get your idea, Sandy. He couldn't interest me. He would be an ignoramus in such things—he would bore me, and I would bore him."

"You have got it. You would bore the patriarchs when you talked, and when they talked they would shoot over your head. By and by you would say, 'Good morning, your Eminence, I will call again' — but you wouldn't. Did you ever ask the slush-boy to come up in the cabin and take dinner with you?"

"I get your drift again, Sandy. I wouldn't be used to such grand people as the patriarchs and prophets, and I would be sheepish and tongue-tied in their company, and mighty glad to get out of it. Sandy, which is the highest rank, patriarch or prophet?"

"Oh, the prophets hold over the patriarchs. The newest prophet, even, is of a sight more consequence than the oldest patriarch. Yes, sir, Adam himself has to walk behind Shakespeare."

"Was Shakespeare a prophet?"

"Of course he was; and so was Homer, and heaps more. But Shakespeare and the rest have to walk behind a common tailor from Tennessee, by the name of Billings; and behind a horse-doctor named Sakka, from Afghanistan. Jeremiah, and Billings and Buddha walk together, side by side, right behind a crowd from planets not in our astronomy; next come a dozen or two from Jupiter and other worlds; next come Daniel, and Sakka and Confucius; next a lot from systems outside of ours; next come Ezekiel, and Mahomet, Zoroaster, and a knife-grinder from ancient Egypt; then there is a long string, and after them, away down toward the bottom, come Shakespeare and Homer, and a shoemaker named Marais, from the back settlements of France."

"Have they really rung in Mahomet and all those other heathens?"

"Yes—they all had their message, and they all get their reward. The man who don't get his reward on earth, needn't bother—he will get it here, sure."

"But why did they throw off on Shakespeare, that way, and put him away down there below those shoe-makers and horse-doctors and knife-grinders—a lot of people nobody ever heard of?"

"That is the heavenly justice of it—they warn't rewarded according to their deserts, on earth, but here they get their rightful rank. That tailor Billings, from Tennessee, wrote poetry that Homer and Shakespeare couldn't begin to come up to; but nobody would print it, nobody read it but his neighbors, an ignorant lot, and they laughed at it. Whenever the village had a drunken frolic and a dance, they would drag him in and crown him with cabbage leaves, and pretend to bow down to him; and one night when he was sick and nearly starved to death, they had him out and crowned him, and then they rode him on a rail about the village, and everybody followed along, beating tin pans and yelling. Well, he died before morning. He wasn't ever expecting to go to heaven, much less that there was going to be any fuss made over him, so I reckon he was a good deal surprised when the reception broke on him."

"Was you there, Sandy?"

"Bless you, no!"

"Why? Didn't you know it was going to come off?"

"Well, I judge I did. It was the talk of these realms—not for a day, like this barkeeper business, but for twenty years before the man died."

"Why the mischief didn't you go, then?"

"Now how you talk! The like of me go meddling around at the reception of a prophet? A mudsill like me trying to push in and help receive an awful grandee like Edward J. Billings? Why, I should have been laughed at for a billion miles around. I shouldn't ever heard the last of it."

"Well, who did go, then?"

"Mighty few people that you and I

will ever get a chance to see, Captain. Not a solitary commoner ever has the luck to see a reception of a prophet, I can tell you. All the nobility, and all the patriarchs and prophets—every last one of them—and all the archangels, and all the princes and governors and viceroys, were there,—and *no* small fry—not a single one. And mind you, I'm not talking about only the grandees from *our* world, but the princes and patriarchs and so on from *all* the worlds that shine in our sky, and from billions more that belong in systems upon systems away outside of the one our sun is in. There were some prophets and patriarchs there that ours ain't a circumstance to, for rank and illustriousness and all that. Some were from

Jupiter and other worlds in our own system, but the most celebrated were three poets, Saa, Bo and Soof, from great planets in three different and very remote systems. These three names are common and familiar in every nook and corner of heaven, clear from one end of it to the other—fully as well known as the eighty Supreme Archangels, in fact—whereas our Moses, and Adam, and the rest, have not been heard of outside of our world's little corner of heaven, except by a few very learned men scattered here and there—and they always spell their names wrong, and get the performances of one mixed up with the doings of another, and they almost always locate them simply *in our solar system*, and think that is enough without going into little details such as naming the particular world they are from. It is like a learned Hindoo showing off how much he knows by saying Longfellow lives in the United States—as if he lived all over the United States, and as if the country was so small you couldn't throw a brick there without hitting him. Between you and me, it does gravel me, the cool way people from those monster worlds outside our system snub our little world, and even our system. Of course we think a good deal of Jupiter, because our world is only a potato to it, for size; but then there are worlds in other systems that Jupiter isn't even a mustard-seed to — like the planet Goobra, for instance, which you couldn't squeeze inside the orbit of Halley's comet without straining the rivets. Tourists from Goobra (I mean parties that lived and died there—natives) come here, now and then, and inquire about our world, and when they find out it is so little that a streak of lightning can flash clear around it in the eighth of a second, they have to lean up against something to laugh. Then they screw a glass into their eye and go to examining *us*, as if we were a curious kind of foreign bug, or something of that sort. One of them asked me how long our day was; and when I told him it was twelve hours long, as a general thing, he asked me if people where I was from considered it worth while to get up and wash for such a day as that.

That is the way with those Goobra people—they can't seem to let a chance go by to throw it in your face that their day is three hundred and twenty-two of our years long. This young snob was just of age—he was six or seven thousand of his days old—say two million of our years—and he had all the puppy airs that belong to that time of life — that turning-point when a person has got over being a boy and yet ain't quite a man exactly. If it had been anywhere else but in heaven, I would have given him a piece of my mind. Well, anyway, Billings had the grandest reception that has been seen in thousands of centuries, and I think it will have a good effect. His name will be carried pretty far, and it will make our system talked about, and maybe our world, too, and raise us in the respect of the general public of heaven. Why, look here—Shakespeare walked backwards before that tailor from Tennessee, and scattered flowers for him to walk on, and Homer stood behind his chair and waited on him at the banquet. Of course that didn't go for much *there*, amongst all those big foreigners from other systems, as they hadn't heard of Shakespeare or Homer either, but it would amount to considerable down there on our little earth if they could know about it. I wish there was something *in* that miserable spiritualism, so we could send them word. That Tennessee village would set up a monument to Billings, then, and his autograph would outsell Satan's. Well, they had grand times at that reception—a small-fry noble from Hoboken told me all about it—Sir Richard Duffer, Baronet."

"What, Sandy, a nobleman from Hoboken? How is that?"

"Easy enough. Duffer kept a sausage-shop and never saved a cent in his life because he used to give all his spare meat to the poor, in a quiet way. Not tramps,—no, the other sort—the sort that will starve before they will beg—honest square people out of work. Dick used to watch hungry-looking men and women and children, and track them home, and find out all about them from the neighbors, and then feed them and find them work. As nobody ever *saw* him give anything to anybody, he had the reputation of being mean; he died with it, too, and everybody said it was a good riddance; but the minute he landed here, they made him a baronet, and the very first words Dick the sausage-maker of Hoboken heard when he stepped upon the heavenly shore were, 'Welcome, Sir Richard Duffer!' It surprised him some, because he thought he had reasons to believe he was pointed for a warmer climate than this one."

All of a sudden the whole region fairly rocked under the crash of eleven hundred and one thunder blasts, all let off at once, and Sandy says,—

"There, that's for the barkeep."

I jumped up and says,—

"Then let's be moving along, Sandy; we don't want to miss any of this thing, you know."

"Keep your seat," he says; "he is only just telegraphed, that is all."

"How?"

"That blast only means that he has been sighted from the signal-station. He is off Sandy Hook. The committees will go down to meet him, now, and escort him in. There will be ceremonies and delays; they won't be coming up the Bay for a considerable time, yet. It is several billion miles away, anyway."

"*I* could have been a barkeeper and a hard lot just as well as not," says I, remembering the lonesome way I arrived, and how there wasn't any committee nor anything.

"I notice some regret in your voice," says Sandy, "and it is natural enough; but let bygones be bygones; you went according to your lights, and it is too late now to mend the thing."

"No, let it slide, Sandy, I don't mind. But you've got a Sandy Hook *here*, too, have you?"

"We've got everything here, just as it is below. All the States and Territories of the Union, and all the kingdoms of the earth and the islands of the sea are laid out here just as they are on the globe—all the same shape they are down there, and all graded to the relative size, only each State and realm and island is a good many billion times bigger here than it is below. There goes another blast."

"What is that one for?"

"That is only another fort answering the first one. They each fire eleven hundred and one thunder blasts at a single dash—it is the usual salute for an eleventh-hour guest; a hundred for each hour and an extra one for the guest's sex; if it was a woman we would know it by their leaving off the extra gun."

"How do we know there's eleven hundred and one, Sandy, when they all go off at once?—and yet we certainly do know."

"Our intellects are a good deal sharpened up, here, in some ways, and that is one of them. Numbers and sizes and distances are so great, here, that we have to be made so we can *feel* them—our old ways of counting and measuring and ciphering wouldn't ever give us an idea of them, but would only confuse us and oppress us and make our heads ache."

After some more talk about this, I says: "Sandy, I notice that I hardly ever see a white angel; where I run across one white angel, I strike as many as a hundred million copper-colored ones—people that can't speak English. How is that?"

"Well, you will find it the same in any State or Territory of the American corner of heaven you choose to go to. I have shot along, a whole week on a stretch, and gone millions and millions of miles, through perfect swarms of angels, without ever seeing a single white one, or hearing a word I could understand. You see, America was occupied a billion years and more, by Injuns and Aztecs, and that sort of folks, before a white man ever set his foot in it. During the first three hundred years after Columbus's discovery, there wasn't ever more than one good lecture audience of white people, all put together, in America—I mean the whole thing, British Possessions and all; in the beginning of our century there were only 6,000,000 or 7,000,000 — say seven; 12,000,000 or 14,000,000 in 1825; say 23,000,000 in 1850; 40,000,000 in 1875. Our death-rate has always been 20 in 1000 per annum. Well, 140,000 died the first year of the century; 280,000 the twenty-fifth year; 500,000 the fiftieth year; about a million the seventy-fifth year.

Now I am going to be liberal about this thing, and consider that fifty million whites have died in America from the beginning up to to-day—make it sixty, if you want to; make it a hundred million—it's no difference about a few millions one way or t'other. Well, now, you can see, yourself, that when you come to spread a little dab of people like that over these hundreds of billions of miles of American territory here in heaven, it is like scattering a ten-cent box of homœopathic pills over the Great Sahara and expecting to find them again. You can't expect us to amount to anything in heaven, and we *don't*—now that is the simple fact, and we have got to do the best we can with it. The learned men from other planets and other systems come here and hang around a while, when they are touring around the Kingdom, and then go back to their own section of heaven and write a book of travels, and they give America about five lines in it. And what do they say about us? They say this wilderness is populated with a scattering few hundred thousand billions of red angels, with now and then a curiously complected *diseased* one. You see, they think we whites and the occasional nigger are Injuns that have been bleached out or blackened by some leprous disease or other—for some peculiarly rascally *sin*, mind you. It is a mighty sour pill for us all, my friend—even the modestest of us, let alone the other kind, that think they are going to be received like a long-lost government bond, and hug Abraham into the bargain. I haven't asked you any of the particulars, Captain, but I judge it goes without saying—if my experience is worth anything — that there wasn't much of a hooraw made over you when you arrived — now was there?"

"Don't mention it, Sandy," says I, coloring up a little; "I wouldn't have had the family see it for any amount you are a mind to name. Change the subject, Sandy, change the subject."

"Well, do you think of settling in the California department of bliss?"

"I don't know. I wasn't calculating on doing anything really definite in that direction till the family come. I thought I would just look around, meantime, in a quiet way, and make up my mind. Besides, I know a good many dead people, and I was calculating to hunt them up and swap a little gossip with them about friends, and old times, and one thing or another, and ask them how they like it here, as far as they have got. I reckon my wife will want to camp in the California range, though, because most all her departed will be there, and sh. likes to be with folks she knows."

"Don't you let her. You see what the Jersey district of heaven is, for whites; well, the Californian district is a thousand times worse. It swarms with a mean kind of leather-headed mud-colored angels—and your nearest white neighbor is likely to be a million miles away. *What a man mostly misses, in heaven, is company* —company of his own sort and color and language. I have come near settling in the European part of heaven once or twice on that account."

"Well, why didn't you, Sandy?"

"Oh, various reasons. For one thing, although you *see* plenty of whites there, you can't understand any of them, hardly, and so you go about as hungry for talk as you do here. I like to look at a Russian or a German or an Italian—I even like to look at a Frenchman if I ever have the luck to catch him engaged in anything that ain't indelicate—but *looking* don't cure the hunger—what you want is talk."

"Well, there's England, Sandy—the English district of heaven."

"Yes, but it is not so very much better than this end of the heavenly domain. As long as you run across Englishmen born this side of three hundred years ago, you are all right; but the minute you get back of Elizabeth's time the language begins to fog up, and the further back you go the foggier it gets. I had some talk with one Langland and a man by the name of Chaucer — old-time poets — but it was no use, I couldn't quite understand them, and they couldn't quite understand me. I have had letters from them since, but it is such broken English I can't make it out. Back of those men's time the English are just simply foreigners, nothing more, nothing less; they talk Danish, German, Norman French, and sometimes a mixture of all three; back of *them*, they talk Latin, and ancient British, Irish, and Gaelic; and then back of these come billions and billions of pure savages that talk a gibberish that Satan himself couldn't understand. The fact is, where you strike one man in the English settlements that you can understand, you wade through awful swarms that talk something you can't make head nor tail of. You see, every country on earth has been overlaid so often, in the course of a billion years, with different kinds of people and different sorts of languages, that this sort of mongrel business was bound to be the result in heaven."

"Sandy," says I, "did you see a good many of the great people history tells about?"

"Yes—plenty. I saw kings and all sorts of distinguished people."

"Do the kings rank just as they did below?"

"No; a body can't bring his rank up here with him. Divine right is a good-enough earthly romance, but it don't go, here. Kings drop down to the general level as soon as they reach the realms of grace. I knew Charles the Second very well—one of the most popular comedians in the English section—draws first rate. There are better, of course—people that were never heard of on earth—but Charles is making a very good reputation indeed, and is considered a rising man. Richard the Lion-hearted is in the prize-ring, and coming into considerable favor. Henry the Eighth is a tragedian, and the scenes where he kills people are done to the very life. Henry the Sixth keeps a religious-book stand."

"Did you ever see Napoleon, Sandy?"

"Often—sometimes in the Corsican range, sometimes in the French. He always hunts up a conspicuous place, and goes frowning around with his arms folded and his field-glass under his arm, looking as grand, gloomy and peculiar as his reputation calls for, and very much bothered because he don't stand as high, here, for a soldier, as he expected to."

"Why, who stands higher?"

"Oh, a *lot* of people *we* never heard of before—the shoemaker and horse-doctor and knife-grinder kind, you know — clodhoppers from goodness knows where, that never handled a sword or fired a shot in their lives —but the soldiership was in them, though they never had a chance to show it. But here they take their right place, and Cæsar and Napoleon and Alexander have to take a back seat. The greatest military genius our world ever produced was a brick-layer from somewhere back of Boston —died during the Revolution—by the name of Absalom Jones. Wherever he goes, crowds flock to see him. You see, everybody knows that if he had had a chance he would have shown the world some generalship that would have made all generalship before look like child's play and 'prentice work. But he never got a chance;

he tried heaps of times to enlist as a private, but he had lost both thumbs and a couple of front teeth, and the recruiting sergeant wouldn't pass him. However, as I say, everybody knows, now, what he *would* have been, and so they flock by the million to get a glimpse of him whenever they hear he is going to be anywhere. Cæsar, and Hannibal, and Alexander, and Napoleon are all on his staff, and ever so many more great generals; but the public hardly care to look at *them* when *he* is around. Boom! There goes another salute. The barkeeper's off quarantine now."

Sandy and I put on our things. Then we made a wish, and in a second we were at the reception-place. We stood on the edge of the ocean of space, and looked out over the dimness, but couldn't make out anything. Close by us was the Grand Stand—tier on tier of dim thrones rising up toward the zenith. From each side of it spread away the tiers of seats for the general public. They spread away for leagues and leagues—you couldn't see the ends. They were empty and still, and hadn't a cheerful look, but looked dreary, like a theatre before anybody comes—gas turned down. Sandy says,—

"We'll sit down here and wait. We'll see the head of the procession come in sight away off yonder pretty soon, now."

Says I,—

"It's pretty lonesome, Sandy; I

reckon there's a hitch somewheres. Nobody but just you and me—it ain't much of a display for the barkeeper."

"Don't you fret, it's all right. There'll be one more gun-fire—then you'll see."

In a little while we noticed a sort of a lightish flush, away off on the horizon.

"Head of the torchlight procession," says Sandy.

It spread, and got lighter and brighter: soon it had a strong glare like a locomotive headlight; it kept on getting brighter and brighter till it was like the sun peeping above the horizon-line at sea—the big red rays shot high up into the sky.

"Keep your eyes on the Grand Stand and the miles of seats—sharp!"

says Sandy, "and listen for the gun-fire."

Just then it burst out, "Boom-boom-boom!" like a million thunder-storms in one, and made the whole heavens rock. Then there was a sudden and awful glare of light all about us, and in that very instant every one of the millions of seats was occupied, and as far as you could see, in both directions, was just a solid pack of people, and the place was all splendidly lit up! It was enough to take a body's breath away. Sandy says,—

"That is the way we do it here. No time fooled away; nobody straggling in after the curtain's up. Wishing is quicker work than travelling. A quarter of a second ago these folks were millions of miles from here. When they heard the last signal, all they had to do was to wish, and here they are."

The prodigious choir struck up,—

> We long to hear thy voice,
> To see thee face to face.

It was noble music, but the uneducated chipped in and spoilt it, just as the congregations used to do on earth.

The head of the procession began to pass, now, and it was a wonderful sight. It swept along, thick and solid, five hundred thousand angels abreast, and every angel carrying a torch and singing—the whirring thunder of the wings made a body's head ache. You could follow the line of the procession back, and slanting upward into the sky, far away in a glittering snaky rope, till it was only a faint streak in the distance. The rush went on and on, for a long time, and at last, sure enough, along comes the barkeeper, and then everybody rose, and a cheer went up that made the heavens shake, I tell you! He was all smiles, and had his halo tilted over one ear in a cocky way, and was the most satisfied-looking saint I ever saw. While he marched up the steps of the Grand Stand, the choir struck up,—

> The whole wide heaven groans,
> And waits to hear that voice."

There were four gorgeous tents standing side by side in the place of honor, on a broad railed platform in the centre of the Grand Stand, with a shining guard of honor round about them. The tents had been shut up all this time. As the barkeeper climbed along up, bowing and smiling to everybody, and at last got to the platform, these tents were jerked up aloft all of a sudden, and we saw four noble thrones of gold, all caked with jewels, and in the two middle ones sat old white-whiskered men, and in the two others a couple of the most glorious and gaudy giants, with platter halos and beautiful armor. All the millions went down on their knees, and stared, and looked glad, and burst out into a joyful kind of murmurs. They said,—

"Two archangels!—that is splendid. Who can the others be?"

The archangels gave the barkeeper

a stiff little military bow; the two old men rose; one of them said, "Moses and Esau welcome thee!" and then all the four vanished, and the thrones were empty.

The barkeeper looked a little disappointed, for he was calculating to hug those old people, I judge; but it was the gladdest and proudest multitude you ever saw—because they had seen Moses and Esau. Everybody was saying, "Did you see them?—I did—Esau's side face was to me, but I saw Moses full in the face, just as plain as I see you this minute!"

The procession took up the barkeeper and moved on with him again, and the crowd broke up and scattered. As we went along home, Sandy said it was a great success, and the barkeeper would have a right to be proud of it forever. And he said *we* were in luck, too; said we might attend receptions for forty thousand years to come, and not have a chance to see a brace of such grand moguls as Moses and Esau. We found afterwards that we had come near seeing another patriarch, and likewise a genuine prophet besides, but at the last moment they sent regrets. Sandy said there would be a monument put up there, where Moses and Esau had stood, with the date and circumstances, and all about the whole business, and travellers would come for thousands of years and gawk at it, and climb over it, and scribble their names on it.

THE END.